THE DOMINION OF LIFE

SAMSON MCCUNE

ISBN-13: 978-1-958401-00-2

Cover art by Samson McCune
Interior design by Samson McCune

Give feedback on the book at:
samsonmccune@gmail.com

First Edition

Printed in the U.S.A

*To Mr. Lorenzoni, who believed in my work ethic and cheered
me on throughout it all.*

Samson McCune

"When the world broke, we tried to fix it and found that it could not be done. For the world was never anything but chaos and pain, dangerously horrid. All we can do is do our best to rule over it."

— Victoria Norgaard

THE FINAL FLICKER

A man sat and watched his last sunset, only vaguely aware of that fact. On his front porch, he rocked in his chair with his dog by his side and a beer in his hand. Inside, his wife, Marie, was playing games with their children as dinner cooked in the oven. It was a warm summer night. Bugs buzzed and birds chirped, reminding the man of how much he missed playing outside as a child.

The yellow sunlight soon changed from its bright hue to a darker, almost malicious, red. The man could tell that something was wrong. The color was wrong, the heat was wrong, the size was wrong, but he loved it still. Always, the sun had been there to embrace him when he needed it most, brightening his life in every way.

His dog likely didn't understand this connection, nor did it have the ability to form complex thoughts, and even so, the man was eternally grateful for the fact that it was sharing that moment with him. It was another thing that brought love and generosity to him, which, like the gifts that had been to him from the sun, he didn't believe he had done enough good to deserve.

The dinner call came a few moments sooner than he would have liked, so he waited and called back, asking if they could perhaps wait for him to finish, with what, he did not elaborate. So they waited, knowing that he was alternatively entertained and would soon be in to join them.

A gust of wind blew into his face, forcing his eyes shut, and when they opened, the sun was gone. The man felt a lump forming in his throat and wondered why he suddenly felt so sad, so lonely. He had not lost any of his loved ones in quite some time, not since his best friend had died in a car accident all of those years ago.

Without making any conscious effort to do so, as his mind was still all too focused on the sunset, the man rose to his feet and retreated into his home where perhaps he could feel some sort of consolation within the embrace of his family. Consolation from what, he didn't know, only understanding that something had served to reduce him to a mess of emotion and nostalgia.

The man was met with the normal laughing and yelling that came with family time, and instead of quieting them down, this time he watched them, capturing the moment as it passed him by. His wife carried the meal to the table: steak and potatoes, with a side of broccoli. The children groaned, begging the man and the woman not to force them to eat the horrid green bits on their plate. The father felt a tear form in his eye as he thought of the childhood innocence in their words.

Perhaps sensing the mood of their father, they ate in an unfamiliar quietude, wondering what had happened to make him feel that way. The night was beautiful and young, and yet, he was acting like he had just seen something that would break the paradigm that their lives had been built upon. The children would never have admitted it to anyone, let alone themselves, but this idea terrified them. They were satisfied with stagnancy so long as it meant more playing in the mud until they got so hungry that they considered eating the mud pies that they had made. So long as it meant that their life was full of happiness and healing.

In those moments of confusion, the children resolved to help their father before bed, hoping that their love and cheer could do something to hide the pain that he was feeling. They, too, felt this ominous sentiment that was overcoming their father, however, their concern for him overshadowed this so it was easy for them to ignore.

They ate quickly, passing easily over their greens, taking small bites of the meat, and focusing on the potatoes. Their mother's gaze told them that she, too, saw what they were seeing, but didn't want to say anything about it. The father had never been the kind of person who talked about his feelings, at least that's what she told them, so they knew it was their job to help him even if he didn't ask them to.

They planned their surprise while their mother and father cleaned up, swept, did the dishes and other various tasks that they understood but had no desire to help with. They simply seemed far too boring, and for that reason, the children could not understand how it helped their parents for them to be momentarily unhappy.

In the living room, beneath the veil of a blanket which they were using as the roof for a pillow fort, they devised a plan that they were certain would cheer up their father. Every single minute detail of the plan was discussed, and from conception to execution, the children knew that with their help, their father would go to bed a happy man.

They rushed to their respective stations, knowing that they would have to be precise and efficient with their movements if they were to succeed. Their hearts beat in their chests, but whether it was from nervousness or excitement, or both, none of them knew.

Before they knew it, the moment of glory arrived and their father and mother walked through the door, slowly and with love in their expressions. Screaming out of joy and relief, the children grabbed the blanket that they were hiding in and ran out of their hiding place to wrap their parents in a warm embrace.

Their parents giggled, holding each other happily. Excited, the children wrapped them tighter and started to push on their legs, wondering if they could join in on the hug as well.

With their legs wrapped so tightly that they couldn't walk, the pushing only forced them to the ground, where they fell in a bundle of laughter. Happy to see that their parents weren't so far away from them any longer, the children jumped in and started to play-fight with them, which soon turned into exhausted cuddling.

Unwilling to let the night end so soon, the mother turned on the nearby TV and switched the channel so that the children's favorite cartoons would be playing. She then deftly set out sleeping areas for each member of the family, the dog included, so that they could sleep comfortably and in each other's company.

As expected, this caused quite the uproar of excitement from the children. They ran around the room, excited at the prospect of being able to stay up late. Had their efforts to cheer up their father worked, then? They didn't know and were quickly forgetting about the issue. More important things had come up.

Before long, this energy dissipated and one by one, the children collapsed, ready to find sleep. There were some initial squabbles about whose spot was whose, and the mother wondered if she had made a mistake, but soon the children relaxed and fell asleep where they were without any further complaint. It was magical, and the mother wondered if she had not developed some sort of divine strength. That was simply unheard of, however, and like the children, she would not complain.

At the center of the solar system, the sun, the light of heaven, collapsed in on itself, smashing all of its mass into an infinitesimal singularity. Its last rays escaped this gravitational well; however, the rest of them were stuck. A black hole had replaced it, stealing all of the joy that it had once presented to the world.

The family soon found sleep in their house, which was now

covered by a dark moon and a blanket of lonely stars. Peacefully, they snored, waiting for the morning and the sunrise that would come with it, unaware of the fact that it would never arrive.

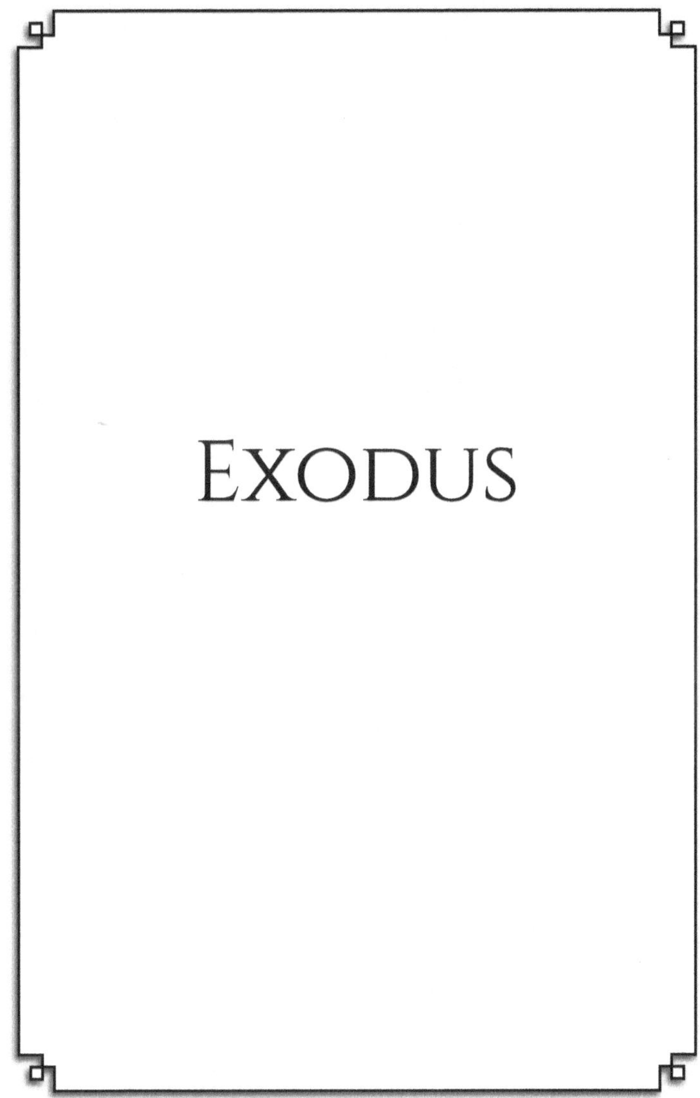

Exodus

-1-

Scott Turner looked out the window of his tiny stateroom, absolutely mystified by what he was seeing. The world was falling around him. On the glass, a translucent reflection of his face stared at him. It was strange how even after the apocalypse he could feel so optimistic and happy. Well, perhaps it wasn't that strange. After all, he was fulfilling his dream of going to space as an engineer.

He checked his bedside clock. 05:45, it read. His smile widened. It was time to go to work. His fellow engineers might think him to be insane, but he didn't care. The work that they were doing was actively preserving the human race, preventing an extinction-level event from ending them. Hell, the fucking sun had just died, something that ancient civilizations had related to the end of all times, and they were still alive. Scott swelled with pride. He was grateful to be a part of something like that.

Quickly he got dressed and gathered his things. Running through the mental list he carried at all times, he finally decided that he had all that he needed, and left.

In the hallway, he passed many people, although most of them were either working in maintenance or engineering. The agricultural workers were on another part of the ship entirely, ensuring that the food supply was above a certain amount at all times. Even they, who sounded foolish and uneducated back on Earth, were playing a massive part in the preservation of life.

It was beautiful, a show of true fellowship. When they had discovered the sun fading, the Country had forgotten its divisions and focused on the problem at hand. Or rather, for the most part. Those who didn't believe in it had stayed behind and those who had come together had provided a chosen few with the means to leave. Now, they were riding aboard one of the many ships containing the last of humanity and the Earth was about to become a ball of ice.

Scott supposed he should have felt lucky for being alive and was curious as to why he didn't. He knew that the selection process had been rigorous and that he had needed to show proficiency in every testable category just to qualify, but still, he didn't feel lucky. He felt that he was where he belonged, finally.

He stopped in front of the entrance to the engineering wing, taking a moment to absorb it all before going in. He could feel his hand jittering and took a deep, calming breath. It was his first day, yes, but he had been selected for a reason. He was going to kick major ass and have a blast doing it.

To his side, a young-looking girl stood, appearing to be admiring the entryway as well. "You too?" he asked, hoping that a conversation would serve to help relieve some of the tension he was feeling.

She looked at him and smiled softly, likely out of courtesy. "Nervousness?"

"Something like that," he chuckled.

"No, I wouldn't say that I feel the same way, then. Although I understand why you would. Presently, my heart has become too overwhelmed by other things for nervousness to find enough room to reside." She paused, and Scott could tell that she was in a great deal of pain. "Maybe one day I can have the privilege of feeling nervous again."

Scott frowned and nodded, unsure of how he was supposed to respond to something like that. Just from their short interaction, it seemed that she was both sad and unwilling to change this fact. He wasn't sure that he could relate to her in the long run, but if she were one of his coworkers, he would work hard to set these feelings aside. He didn't believe in snap judgments.

"Our waiting is bordering on weird," he chuckled. "They probably think that we're stalking them, hoping to steal their engineering secrets."

Surprisingly, the woman laughed as well. Where had all of her grief gone? "Engineers can be the most pretentiously humble people, can't they."

"Most certainly," Scott replied. "They always say that they will be the ones to change the world and frame it as if they are just following their passion and not doing it at least partially for the glory."

"Are you?"

"Doing it for the glory?"

She nodded.

He furrowed his brow. "To an extent, I guess. The difference is I don't want to change the world anymore. I just want to experience it."

She tilted her head and nodded again, almost to say that she approved of him and the things that he had said. Then she pushed her way through the entrance, not waiting to see whether or not Scott would follow her in.

Scott had almost immediately lost the woman and instead of following her, he had gone to where he was supposed to be working. There, he had set his things down and started working. He had already been trained, so there was no confusion about what he was supposed to do, but there was still a part of him that wondered why he was doing what he did. All he had to do was check acceleration data, fuel levels, and breaches in airlocks. Most of it sounded like maintenance grunt work. Not that he was complaining, he just wasn't sure how his education and training came into play.

After a few moments of intense work, a glance told him that he was the only person working. Everyone else was staring at the front of the room, where the woman that he had met before was standing.

"I am Commander Norgaard," she began. "Today, we begin our great migration, headed to a new world which will carry many unknowns and many possibilities. Things will go wrong between our arrival and now. In fact, I can assure you that a great many things will go wrong. People will get hurt. They will die."

Scott wished she would stop being so pessimistic. Was she really trying to hype them up with something so upsetting to hear?

"But that is why we have you," she said as she pointed to her audience, of which Scott was a member. "Our corps of engineers, the most brilliant minds that haven't left us. The protectors of order, of safety, of all that is keeping life in our solar system. In this way, you people have been granted the gift of divinity. You are the people who will decide who will live and who will die. Your lives and your passions are the heart of this ship, and without you, we would be lost and dead."

Scott blinked. That was quite a shift, although the tone hadn't changed much.

"Don't let the hopes and dreams of your loved ones die with us," she continued, a tear forming in her eye now. "When the sun went out, its light was thrust upon you. Carry it with pride."

Scott felt a lump forming in his throat. Where had that come from? Had her speech truly touched him so much that it had made him feel emotional? That was new.

Not sure how to process these new feelings, Scott got back to work, this time unquestioningly. His work might have been largely maintenance, but that was why he was the one doing it. They had no room for mistakes. Everything had to work perfectly, or further catastrophe would come. He was a champion for order and nature, the champion of discord. Locked in their battle, they would fight until discord won. Scott was not so foolish as to think that anything else would happen. He knew that he was the one to extend the stalemate as long as possible, though. *If I wasn't doing it for the glory before, I might be now,* he thought, silently cursing Commander Norgaard for her speaking abilities.

-2-

The world was ending. What to do, some people thought they knew, although Scott believed their confidence was unfounded. Or rather, he figured that they were unaware of how to truly solve the problem. Sure, there were theories around warp drives and going to other planets, but all of them required an insane amount of resources that he found hard to believe existed.

So far, the United States government had been the only nation to have officially recognized the threat, claiming that its data was indicating that there would be the birth of a black hole. Scott didn't understand this as there wasn't enough mass for that to happen, and even if there were, he was fairly certain that for there to be a black hole, a supernova had to happen first. And from what he had heard, the sun wasn't expanding, but rather beginning its collapse.

There was so much happening that nobody understood, and as a result, the scientific community had begun to blame dark energy. Scientists rapidly expanded their research of other, more distant stars, and soon discovered the existence of other celestial bodies that were undergoing, or had undergone similar processes.

Personally, Scott thought that it was all bullshit. It was confirmation bias at best, and at worst, the scientific community was lying to the world so that they could cover their asses. He knew them well enough to know that being able to say 'I don't know,' was not a very common trait. They all, or at least the prominent ones, were far too interested in the fame and glory that they didn't want to be known as the person who didn't act. He supposed he understood their aversion to complacency, but the idea that not making a mistake was worse than purposefully getting the problem wrong didn't sit well with him.

And he didn't have any proof of these ideas anyway; they were all conjecture. However, he felt that this was the same way the scientific community was operating. Theories could only go so far.

In the end, he guessed it didn't matter what the origin of the event was, at least not in the short term. The only thing that mattered was that it was happening, and they needed to find a way to either reverse it or prevent the total extinction of life from Earth.

Scott set his phone down and pinched the bridge of his nose. So much bad news in just a few articles. He wished they would have presented a solution. Just like that, the world had changed in tone. They had always known that it was going to end soon, but the difference was that in the past, they knew humans were going to be the cause. He wondered if it was odd that he wished that that would have happened instead.

Nature wasn't supposed to betray them. His entire life, he had studied how to mimic the brilliance of nature, but humans had never even come close. They could copy and paste life, burn things for energy, and move at incredible speeds, but these things were nothing compared to what the universe had just become able to do. With evolution, it had birthed the human mind, with nuclear physics it had made stars, and with subatomic particle physics, it had made light.

Helen walked into the kitchen with a loud yawn. Scott squinted at the windows and saw that the sun had been up for a few hours. Had he stayed up all night reading?

"Why are you up?" Helen asked groggily as she opened the fridge.

"I couldn't sleep," Scott replied, unsure whether or not he should tell his roommate what he had just spent hours researching.

"That sucks." Scott could hear jars and containers colliding as she searched for things to make her breakfast. "I had the craziest dream. Wanna hear about it?"

"Sure."

"Walt and Sydney were with me in the pool, right? Or wait, no, it actually started earlier. I was back in high school and for some reason, Walt and Sydney were with me. They wanted to go…"

Scott nodded along, barely recognizing what she was saying. He could hear the beats in her tone, though, and knew when to respond physically to make it seem like he was listening. But why should he listen? Why did it matter? Everything that he had worked for, every reason that he had pushed himself so far, was about to disappear. Was there even a reason to live anymore if everyone was just going to die?

"Are you even listening?" Helen asked, her words piercing through his mental fog.

Scott didn't know what to say. He felt a lump forming in his throat. Where had the time gone? When had the world decided that it would end? Why was it all happening?

Helen opened her mouth and spoke to him again, but he wasn't listening. His vision blurry and his chest in pain, Scott Turner, the last of his family, started to weep. Hopelessness had overtaken even him, the carrier of the light.

-3-

BEEP. BEEP. BEEP. Scott awoke with a jolt, looking for the source of the horrendous noise. **BEEP. BEEP. BEEP.** "Shut the fuck up," he said groggily as he got up from his desk, fumbling with random objects around him with the hopes that one of them might end the pain in his ears. **BEEP. BEEP. BEEP.**

Finally, a random switch nearby silenced the noise and he was blessed by a beautiful peace. It took him a moment to re-configure himself around his surroundings, but when he did, he noticed scientists had worked to create artificial lighting that could reproduce a natural circadian rhythm but for some reason, it had little to no effect on him, and in his fatigued daze, he wondered why time even mattered.

As he woke up, his mind accelerated back towards the beeping. Yes, of course. The beeping. "What the hell was that?" he thought aloud as he looked for the switch with hopes that it might have just been some random alarm.

But he knew better than that. The ships were designed for efficiency and accuracy, meaning that an alarm of that volume and pitch would not have been allowed aboard. Something was wrong. Scott wiped the last licks of sleep from his eyes and focused his efforts on finding the source of the problem.

"Is it strange that I regret turning that switch off now?" he asked himself, chuckling in frustrated astonishment. He flipped books and checked under desks and tables, but no matter how much he looked, he couldn't seem to find whatever switch or lever had been hit.

If it had been a different time, a better time, Scott would have been interested in the idea of the difference between the physical and visual registration of objects in the mind, but he was far too preoccupied currently to spare any effort to think about anything except thinking about it.

No matter how hard he tried, though, he could not locate anything even remotely similar to the switch. It was as if it had appeared to irritate him and disappeared to irk him even more. It was a poetic thought, but unhelpful.

Frustrated, Scott sat back down and slammed his head against the table.

BEEP. BEEP. BEEP.

He shot up. There it was! Never had he thought that he would have been so happy to hear the most ear-splitting, brain-splattering noise that had ever been made in human history, but there he was, grinning like an idiot.

Now all he had to do was find out where it was coming from and for what purpose. **BEEP. BEEP. BEEP.** A part of him was expecting the search for the source to be as annoying as the search for the lever, and he was glad to be immediately proven wrong. On a display at the front of the room, there was a red triangle with an error message flashing below it.

He wove his way through tables and chairs to get a better look. **ERROR CODE 764576**, it read. Scott racked his brain, trying to remember which one that was. He wished there hadn't been quite so many things that could go wrong but guessed that that was the price to be paid with a complex spaceship.

He started pacing back and forth, hoping that he was just being slow because he was tired and not stupid when an anamoly caught his eye. On a desk nearby, there was a magnetic levitator. The object being magnetically suspended was supposed to be stationary but it wasn't. It was rising, and soon it fell to the floor. What was going on? Taking another step, he suddenly felt lighter as well.

Eyes widening with an immediate understanding, Scott ran and checked the trajectory estimator for the voyage. Sure enough, what had previously been a countdown to impact with Jupiter was now a loading screen, helplessly recalculating to find a time that he knew would never come.

At least one of the engines had stopped working.

Scott took a deep breath and tried to think. He needed to tell someone. Commander Norgaard would want to know. His coworkers, whose names he had never cared to learn, would want to know as well. Hell, everyone on the ship would want to now. But it wasn't time to tell them yet. He still had some calculations to do.

Before he did that, he checked the computer to see if it would simply tell him what exactly had happened and why. The pure data would have been much appreciated. As he suspected, though, something deeper was wrong and the computer was only able to tell that the accelerometer wasn't receiving the correct input. Oddly, it wasn't able to tell him what its input was, but that was a problem for another time.

First, he did what he was going to call the 'feel test.' Now, the feel test was incredibly precise, taking into account a great many variables, such as pressure, acceleration, time, and impulse. He jumped. It didn't feel too wrong, and he didn't feel like he was jumping too high, which was a good sign. He performed a few more trials of the feel test, but as he had expected, each trial gave him very similar results.

He took note of this while also taking the time to notate the desired acceleration value as '10.' This was relatively close to 9.8, or 1 g, which was the actual value for gravity, but 10 was easier to work with so he stuck with it. Looking over his data, he knew that it was time for a Fermi Approximation.

Scott laughed at himself for thinking of something like that.

He had often, in the past, thought of Fermi Approximations as calculations to do when the majority of the problem was unknown, meaning that the solution reached would always be at least slightly wrong. He knew that they had a purpose, but the perfectionist in him hated this fact and frequently elected to ignore it. Oh, how the tables had turned.

With the upper bound of gravity being 10, Scott decided that a simple initial lower bound would be 0, although he knew with certainty that this was false. That was the point, though: making adjustments until the bounds closed around the actual value.

It wasn't at 5, that was still too low. He had trained in acceleration pods and knew that half of a g was surprisingly different from 1 g, so he raised it again. For a reason that he couldn't understand, he settled on .75 g's for his lower bound. It felt right. Why? He had no idea. He didn't have perfect accelerational pitch so that he could tell someone how many gs he was feeling at any given moment, but .75 still seemed like the safest and most correct answer.

This meant that the amount of time that it would take for them to get to Jupiter would increase by something like 30%. That didn't sound so bad at first, however, Scott remembered that going to Jupiter wasn't like a road trip. Their destination was actively *moving*, meaning that it wasn't a trip, but rather an interception. And with their current acceleration, they were going to miss.

-4-

"So how long have you been experiencing this anxiety that you speak of?" Dr. Parten asked from her chair.

Scott took a moment to think, although he knew the answer before she had even finished asking the question. "Ever since… the news."

Dr. Parten tensed slightly at his words but didn't say anything. Apparently having feelings wasn't allowed for a therapist. "Do you know why this is affecting you in this way? Is it perhaps a fear of death, or do you think that it's maybe something else?"

"It's a combination of the two, I think."

"Tell me more about that."

Scott bit at a flap of skin on the inside of his cheek. He had been gnawing on it for days. "I'm not sure if I'm ready to talk about that," he said at last.

Dr. Parten set her notepad down and looked at him with what he could only describe as artificial concern. "Would you like me to be frank or would you like me to help you feel better?"

"Aren't you supposed to do a bit of both?"

"Yes, I am. I was just checking to make sure that it was okay with you."

Scott frowned. Had she not been doing that the whole time?

"If you don't open up about this now, you may never have time to. Now, I'm not telling you that you need to, and by all means, if it makes you too uncomfortable to talk about, don't. However, I implore you to push through, to give yourself the gift of brutal honesty before you move on. I think you'll find it to be freeing."

He knew that she was going to say something like that. And as much as she claimed that there was no pressure to talk, he felt that there was. What if he chose not to continue? She would judge him and continuously bring it up, throwing it at him during his darkest times with claims about how it would only make things better.

Scott laughed in frustration. When had he gotten so cynical? Of course, she was right. Reluctantly, although not as reluctantly as before, Scott opened his mouth and began to speak.

"I grew up in a sort of middle-class family. Not the kind that has great things, but the kind that has been fractured by lost love and broken promises. It wasn't great, but it certainly wasn't terrible. There were parts that I hated, although up until June 6th, 2006, I would say that I lived as normal a life as a child of divorced parents could live."

"Why that day, specifically?"

"It broke me," Scott said simply. "After it, I wasn't the same. I couldn't see things the way they were supposed to be seen. All of the good things in the world lost their flavor, becoming dull and unappealing."

"You were depressed."

"Deeply. Suicide was often on my mind. The release appealed to me, but only in the short term. I truly believe that the only thing that saved me was my belief that I would one day get better."

"Hope is a powerful thing."

Scott stared at his feet and nodded, all too aware of the fact that he had none left. "Yes it is," he said softly. "I'm not sure when I started to feel better, but I did. I don't even remember how or why I did. All I know is that slowly, day by day, my depressive tendencies became less and less common. Life was fine, maybe even good."

"And you're struggling with that depression coming back?"

Scott ignored her. "My joyful attitude was a ray of light. It helped those around me who were struggling with similar problems, and before I knew it, there were people who relied on me to be their source of happiness.

"It hurt me more than they saw. It hurt me more than they could have ever known. But that was the point, I guess. They were never supposed to see that the knives they were tearing out of their bodies were being flung onto mine.

"I made promises to these people with the hopes that things might one day get better for us all, that we could live in peace. That day never came. Slowly, sure enough, they were removed from my life in one way or another, and at the end, I was left to remain a ray of light with nothing to fuel it."

Scott froze, astounded by all that he had just said. Had it been too much? Definitely. Or wait. Maybe not? He couldn't tell how he was feeling.

"And you're worried that you don't have enough time to fulfill your promises?"

Scott checked his watch and stood up. They had fifteen minutes left in their session. "It looks like our time is up," he said quickly as he grabbed his things and left before he could tell her that she was exactly right.

-5-

Scott stood awkwardly outside of Norgaard's stateroom. He had already knocked three times. Would a fourth do him any good? It was too important of an issue for it to be left alone. But what if she was a really heavy sleeper? Could he pick the lock to get in and tell her? How was he supposed to even go about doing that?

He started to panic, unsure of what to do. He wasn't equipped to handle a problem like this on his own. There was supposed to be a chain of command that could tackle catastrophes, and so far as he could see, it had completely disappeared.

"What are you doing outside of my room?" Scott heard from behind him.

Confused, he turned and saw Norgaard standing with a tablet tucked under her arm and a cup of coffee.

"Why aren't you asleep?" Scott asked, feeling slightly foolish.

"You're awake," Norgaard smirked. "Do you even know what time it is?"

Scott shook his head. She showed him his watch. "Technically, it's the morning," she told him. It read 06:45. "What's the issue?"

He searched for the right words, trying to capture the significance of the error.

"Spit it out," she said impatiently.

Scott took a deep breath. "I believe one of our engines failed. Based on a few tests, it seems that our acceleration has decreased by at most 25%."

Norgaard's eyes grew wide.

"Which means that we won't make it to Jupiter."

"I know what it means!" she yelled as she ran over to the wall. She clicked a few buttons and a touch screen appeared. She clicked a few more buttons and then yelled into what he could only assume to be a microphone.

"This is Commander Norgaard! I need every engineer, every programmer, every possible free hand with the tiniest understanding of this ship to report to the engineering hall. NOW!"

Without pausing a moment, she turned and ran down the hall. Scott felt his heart beating in his chest. What if he was wrong? Well, it was better to be safe than sorry, as the saying went. He just wasn't sure if anyone would ever forgive him for the panic that was about to ensue.

To say the room was packed was an understatement. Scott hadn't even been aware that the ship was carrying that many people, let alone people that fulfilled the qualifiers that Norgaard had mentioned. Some appeared to be anxious, while others looked calm and confident. The array of emotions that Scott could see was astounding, although he knew they were all scared out of their minds.

"It has been brought to my attention that our dear vessel is malfunctioning," Norgaard started from where she stood at the front of the room. "Scott, would you like to come up and explain what led you to this conclusion?"

Suddenly, everyone turned their attention toward him. With discomfort and fatigue, Scott moved to join Norgaard.

"Yes. Hi," he said nervously. "Just a few hours ago, I was working in this room when an alarm went off."

A few people called out things like 'what was the error

code?' and 'did you check the computer?' but Scott ignored them and continued.

"Other than an obscure error code that I couldn't understand at the time, there was no indication as to what was wrong. I saw a magnetically levitated object rising and felt lighter, so my initial reaction was that the accelerometer was telling me that something was wrong. I later confirmed this with something called the 'feel test,' which told me that it is likely that we are currently operating at about 80% of the desired acceleration."

The room went silent. All complaints and whispers of dissent had vanished.

"And at this acceleration, we cannot make it to Jupiter," he said after a pause.

"Yes, exactly," Norgaard cut in quickly. "Which means that we must act with extreme haste. We must first identify the source of the problem, and then we must work around the clock to fix it. Am I understood?"

Her words were met with nods all around the room. It was incredible how well problems united people, especially those with an engineering background.

-6-

Scott was dreading the arrival of his friends. He knew that that wasn't what he was supposed to be feeling, however there it was, invading his thoughts and feelings, preventing him from being able to relax. The only thing he could think about was his therapy session earlier that day and how horribly vulnerable and broken he had felt. No matter what Dr. Parten said, that wasn't a good feeling; not even close.

He wished that the world wouldn't change so fast, that it would first give him time to enjoy and adjust before moving on to other things. He figured that was how most people felt when they learned that their days were numbered. It seemed natural.

Even just a week prior, he was spending his time working on a few passion projects, applying for jobs, and getting the courage to ask out a cute girl he saw every morning when he went out for his daily walk. All of that, which had only been seven days before, suddenly felt like it hadn't been relevant for centuries. The sun's disappearance had consumed his life.

If it had had the same effect on Helen, he had no idea. She was still acting like her normal self. On the weekdays she read and scrolled through her computer for 'work,' although he was very well aware of the fact that she was unemployed, and on the weekends she partied. During the time that Scott had known her, those had been the only consistent parts of her life.

"Are you excited to see Walt?" she asked from the kitchen, where she was preparing their usual meat and cheese platter.

"I guess so," Scott replied sullenly.

"When's the last time you guys hung out, anyway?"

"A few weeks ago, if I had to guess. I can't really remember."

"I wonder why he's gotten so distant," Helen said. "Just a few days ago, he was his normal, cheery self, and now he's acting like we don't exist."

Scott had to stop himself from telling her that it was probably because the goddamn world was ending.

"Yeah, I've noticed that, too," he said instead. "I was surprised that he even accepted your invite tonight."

"I'd bet money that he only accepted because I invited Rachel," Helen laughed.

"You're probably right," Scott responded, faking the fact that he was entertained. It was so hard to pretend to care, but he did so anyway. Oddly enough, it felt impolite to sulk about the end of almost all life on Earth.

Helen looked anxiously at the clock. "It's already 6:03," she said. "They were supposed to be here already."

Suddenly, Scott felt as if he understood his roommate. He wasn't sure why, but that tiny gesture had revealed more than weeks of conversation. She was afraid as well, she just wasn't showing it. Staying in her normal routine must have been her way of coping.

"They'll be here," Scott reassured her. "Just give them a bit. There might have been traffic."

"Right," Helen said as her gaze became more and more vacant. "That's what it must be. Traffic."

"Yeah. Don't worry. They'll come."

He heard a knock on their front door.

"There they are!" Scott said with an enthusiastic clap as he shot to his feet. "I'll go let them in. You can stay and finish up."

Visibly happier, Helen started to work faster, cleaning off cutting boards and knives. Trying to mirror her air of energy, Scott feigned happiness as he bounded towards their front door. Admittedly, he was excited to see Walt. They had been friends for years, and it felt like longer since they had had a good time together.

With a grin, he opened the door.

"Scott Turner?" a stranger in a black suit asked.

"You're not Walt," Scott said, confused. "Who are you?"

"My name is Adam. You have been selected by the United States government to partake in the Exodus Project. This is an incredibly important mission that will decide the fate of humanity. Should you accept our offer, you may come with me where you will be briefed further. However, nobody is forcing you to, and should you reject, a waitlist a million strong will shift up one to replace you."

Scott blinked. "The Exodus Project? What is that?"

"Unfortunately, that information is classified. However, if you would like to learn more, you can come with me. I cannot give you further details at this time."

"How am I supposed to know if I want to do something if I don't even know what it is?"

"Do you have a reason to say no?" Adam asked.

Scott took a moment to think, trying to procure some sort of counterargument but found that Adam was right. There was no reason to say no. He was going to die in a few days anyway, just like everyone else.

"No," he said at last.

"Do you accept my offer, then?"

Scott took one last look inside.

"You can't tell her that you're leaving," Adam cut in. "Or anyone for that matter. We can't have people asking questions."

Scott nodded. "That makes sense," he said softly. "When are we leaving?"

"Now."

One last look inside. Scott's chest ached with the knowledge that he would never see his friends again. Was it worth it to leave without saying goodbye? His heart told him yes. As with most other things in his life, his curiosity pushed him on without regret.

Scott closed the door behind him and followed Adam out of the building. "Will I be able to come back and get my things?" he asked.

"You'll get new things," Adam responded shortly, increasing his pace to slightly below a jog.

"But it won't be the same," Scott argued. "I have a retainer, and I left my phone."

Adam increased his speed once more so that they were practically running and pulled them into a car just outside of the building. "Stop complaining!" he yelled. "You'll live!"

"What? Yeah. I know, these aren't big problems. I just would prefer to avoid the inconvenience if possible."

Adam glared at Scott with hatred and jealousy. "That's not what I mean. You get to live. That's the point of this. When the sun breathes its last breath, you won't. You've been chosen to survive."

Scott's eyes widened as a grin formed on his face. "What?" he asked, awestruck.

"The government has a list of specific individuals in case certain... situations come to fruition. Needless to say, you were very high on this list. As a result, you have been picked to be one of the people to lead humanity into its next age."

"So I won't die?"

"Not yet, at least."

Scott cheered so loudly that he thought his lungs were going to burst. The relief that he felt was immeasurable. Never had he felt so euphoric. So grateful to be alive. He took a few calming breaths and was interrupted by his own intermittent laughter.

Adam frowned.

"Sorry. It's just that that is literally the best news I have ever received."

Adam's frown evolved into a horrid scowl. He turned his eyes to the road and put on a pair of dark sunglasses. "I hate my fucking job," the agent whispered.

Scott cackled. It felt good to be alive. It felt good to have something to look forward to. It felt good to have hope.

-7-

People shouted across the room. What appeared to be a chaotic mess was actually an incredibly efficient engine of change. Already, they had fixed a few glitches with the computer and were well on their way to discovering why their systems hadn't worked properly. It was incredible to watch.

The programmers were the main group of people currently working, although Scott could tell that a shift was coming. The further along the software debugging got, the closer the engineers got to being able to do their work.

Scott wasn't much of a programmer, so he didn't have a high level of understanding of what was going on on the software side. People were typing furiously and swearing when things didn't work. He wondered if it was strange that this made him feel slightly better about his coding skills. Before, he had just assumed that he was the only one who could never get their code to do what he wanted it to.

"I wonder if perhaps the ship just malfunctioned," Luc, one of the members of Scott's team whispered to him. "They can't seem to figure out how to fix the error, so is there a chance that the error was with the error reading technology?"

"That almost sounds paradoxical," Scott replied. "If there is an error with the error reading technology, wouldn't we just think that everything is working properly? My gut tells me that most of the error reads were false and only this part told it to us as it was."

"I'm not sure I agree. Is there a chance that instead of throwing a false negative, the program was returning false positives? From what we're looking at here, that seems to be more likely than you say."

"Perhaps." It was annoying to argue back and forth with people without providing any evidence, so Scott chose to ignore Luc. The man had some good points, sure, however, they weren't benefitting anybody. All they were doing was giving them more data to consider when they were already having a hard time managing the information they had.

"Should I go tell the programmers?" Luc asked.

"I'm sure they've already considered everything you're about to tell them," Scott responded with a sigh. "Remember, that's their job. One of them can do more with software in five minutes than all of the engineers together could do in a week."

"I've heard coding is mostly copying and pasting shit from the internet," Luc scowled.

"And if it is, then they're the best there are at pressing control c and control v."

Of course, Scott wasn't a complete degenerate when it came to software development. He had been required to take a few classes related to that in college, and it had come up a few times after, but he had never been able to practice it enough to become truly proficient. He at least knew enough to know that Luc was wrong about what it took to be a programmer.

"Maybe I should just go and check anyway. Communication is important during times of crisis."

Scott squeezed his fist in frustration. It wasn't the time to be annoying or fueled by ego. He wasn't sure why Luc was the only person who couldn't understand that. The rest of his team was sitting quietly, waiting patiently for their turn to pitch in, as was expected of them.

"Yeah. I'm just gonna go and check that girl's tablet," Luc said as he got into a crouch and started to tip-toe over to the other table. "Maybe they're missing some important information."

Scott drew in a quick breath. "Luc, if her tablet moves so much as a millimeter, I'm firing you from my team. If you have a problem with that, you can take it up with Norgaard. Do you understand?"

Luc glared and stalked off. How had they gotten someone like him to embark on the mission? From what little Scott had seen of him, he could already tell that the man was not a team player and cared more about being the one to say something than contributing to the solution of a problem.

"What was that about?" Samantha, another member of his team, asked.

"He doesn't approve of my methods."

"Which are?"

"Staying out of their way until it's time for us to step in."

"He probably thinks that he knows how to solve the problem," Samantha replied.

"He'd be wrong about that."

"I think everyone agrees with you there. I just sometimes wonder what's going through his head."

That interested Scott. "Why do you say that?"

"The two of us have been working together since yesterday, and he just seems erratic is all. There are times when we have to do things because it's protocol, and he finds the strangest things to be problematic. Like why did he sign up for this if he wasn't going to be able to listen to directions every once in a while?"

Scott nodded. "Do you feel that his behavior is concerning enough that it should be reported to one of the higher-ups?"

"Maybe?" Samantha said with an uncertain shrug. "He doesn't feel like he has malintent, though. I just think he might have bad ideas."

"If I see anything else about him that concerns me or if another person says that he is being insubordinate, I'm reporting him. We can't have people like that in positions of power, especially not during times of emergency."

"Agreed," Samantha said quickly.

"We got it!" one of the programmers shouted triumphantly.

Scott's annoyance towards Luc immediately dematerialized. "What was it?" he asked as he rushed over to where she was sitting.

"Essentially, something happened to disable one of the five thrusters, leaving us at about 80% of our expected acceleration," she explained. "On top of that, there were a bunch of problems with our error detection programs, and they weren't able to properly relay this information to the computer in this room."

So he had been right after all, then. "Can we fix this by updating the software?"

The programmer shook her head. "No, because the brilliant engineers of these beautiful vessels didn't want the ships to be able to be launched remotely, they made the engine locks so that they have to be opened manually.

"Which means…"

"Which means that somebody is going to have to do a spacewalk," the programmer said with perhaps the most amount of false enthusiasm that Scott had ever heard.

-8-

It turned out that second chances looked almost as incredible as they felt. The facility that Adam had taken Scott to was nothing if not brilliantly scientific and extravagant at the same time. The entire area reminded him of those houses that he frequently saw online but couldn't afford.

"This is the Kytos Complex," Adam explained. "After a brief orientation, you will be granted full access to anything and everything here, except for a select few areas that you probably won't even notice exist."

"What is this?" Scott found himself asking. It was such a simple question and he felt like quite a fool for not having asked it earlier.

"What do you mean?"

"What even is the Exodus Project?"

"I could tell you, but wouldn't you rather take a tour and see for yourself?"

Scott looked at him flatly. "If you told me, then I wouldn't need a tour and I could get working on what they need me to do more quickly. Would you really prefer some dramatic tension to efficiency?"

Adam grinned maliciously. "Yes. I would."

Scott scowled. He hated when logic didn't prevail. It was clear that the other man was just trying to get under his skin, and he was ashamed to admit that it was working—quite well, at that.

"Ah! Right on time!" Adam said cheerfully after seeing a small old woman from where they were standing in the courtyard. "Your guide has arrived and it is now my time to go and discover another victim to subject to the cruel punishment of a tour!"

He cackled loudly as he walked away. That was a side of Adam that Scott had not expected to see. It was oddly refreshing if he was being honest; normally government workers didn't do anything to prove that they were quite so human.

"Hello there, young sir," the woman croaked upon arrival. She wore an old, satisfied smile that Scott assumed came with age and experience. "My name is Eve. Are you ready for a tour of our facilities?"

Scott groaned. "I don't need a tour. A pamphlet would suffice."

"I'm sorry, sir, but a tour is protocol."

"Could I speak to a boss or a manager?"

"Unfortunately not, sir. People have tried to avoid the tour before and have experienced severe punishment."

Scott clenched his jaw with agitation. If there was one thing he hated, it was being in the dark. That was the problem with being so curious, he supposed; he hated being ignorant when the opposite was possible.

"May I ask why a tour is required?"

Eve's face fell. "You may not."

"Is it that serious?" Scott was taken aback. The old woman had seemed so sweet and patient, yet he had ruined her sunny disposition with one odd question. How had that happened? Or rather, why? It seemed so out of left field.

In silence, she led them through the futuristic courtyard, which appeared to be just that. He had expected there to be technology that was going to blow him away, but trees were still just trees. Humanity hadn't done anything about that yet. Not that it even wanted to.

They stopped at the wall that surrounded the courtyard.

"This yard is perhaps the most controversial part of this entire facility," she began. "As is true with most of the buildings you'll later see, this facility is relatively young: not even 40 years old. The original architect, a man known as Kytos, claimed that a courtyard served to reinforce nature in the lives of humans, even as they jumped into metal boxes and dove into a sea of stars. Some believe he was a hippy, and this could have been done without, however, the majority of the people who have lived here will say that the courtyard is by far the best part."

She led them to a door against the wall and held it open for him. Perhaps she didn't completely hate him after all, then. The inside was sparsely decorated, reminding Scott more of a hospital than the beauty that could be seen throughout the rest of the area.

"This building, Gallahad Hall, is the only place in the entire facility that was not designed entirely by Kytos," Eve said, stopping them in the center of a room that looked eerily similar to a waiting room in a doctor's office.

"It shows," Scott muttered. From what little he had heard about the man, Kytos seemed like he was a visionary architect. "What was it? A decommissioned children's hospital?"

This earned him a glare from Eve, not that he cared. He had already determined that she hated him. "No, actually. It has always been used for the express purpose of housing the people who study here."

"Study here?" Scott perked. "That means that this place is largely used for research, then?"

Eve ignored him and took them through a drearily boring hallway in Gallahad Hall. The more Scott stared at the monochrome of the walls, the more he was reminded of his time in school. Immediately, he felt some of his motivation to learn fade. It was fascinating how much of an impact the past had on the future.

The Dominion of Life

At some point, the style of architecture changed drastically, and Scott's boredom faded. Unlike most walls, which were entirely flat, the ones that he was staring at were composed of hundreds, if not thousands of rectangular prisms, all of different sizes and depths, giving the hallway a sort of sharp, layered texture.

"These halls were part of Kytos' first additions to the complex," Eve explained as they walked. "He truly believed in the idea that life imitated art, and worked hard to make certain that every aspect of his creation was pure art for the purpose of inspiration."

The further they walked, the more abstract the wall became. Scott wondered how something so complex and beautiful could have been built in only 40 years. It seemed like it would take hundreds, if not thousands, even with the right team of people. There was simply an incredible amount of detail present.

"Am I allowed to ask questions?" Scott asked, the thought finally occurring to him that she might only be cold because he wasn't instigating conversation.

"So long as they are relevant and intelligent questions," she said with what Scott could only assume to be a hint of irritation.

"I learned that there is no such thing as an unintelligent question."

"Whoever taught you that was a fool and should have thought before giving you such ignorant advice," Eve said coolly. "The world is full of unintelligent questions. More than you could even imagine."

And at that moment, Scott could see the symptoms of burnout plastered on her face. She was old, probably in her 70s, and was having to deal with a snarky man in his early 30s. He would have been frustrated, too. She probably wanted to be back at home, spending time with her family as opposed to listening to his immature and rude comments.

"I apologize if I have done anything to offend you," he said with an apologetic bow. "If there is anything I can do to help you relay the necessary information to me, please, let me know. I was only acting so childish because I was annoyed by how cryptic things seem to be around here."

Ever stopped where she was standing and turned to look at him. Her face softened and the smile he had first seen her wearing returned, if only slightly. "Your apology means a lot. I appreciate it and thank you for considering my feelings. I'm sure you could see just how tiring this is."

"I can. Perhaps it would be best if you went and took a break and I asked for another guide?"

Eve shook her head. "No, I need the money. I thank you for your concern, though. Shall we continue?"

"If you feel up for it," Scott said, waving for her to lead the way once more.

She hobbled onward. He couldn't have been certain, but it looked like she was slightly limping. He wondered what that might have been about.

The further they went, the more enthralling the buildings became. They passed the dining hall, which was far prettier than Gallahad Hall, a few conference rooms, and the bathrooms, which Scott had happily used. It had been hours since he had been allowed to relieve himself, and he couldn't tell if it just felt good because of how long it had been or because of the complements of the architecture, but it was one of the best pee breaks that he had ever taken.

With a sort of finality about her actions, Eve stopped them in front of a building with the label 'Exodus' on it. It felt like it had been ages since his last conversation with Adam and even longer since he had seen Helen. *What have these last few days even been?* he thought.

"I know you've been dying to learn about this," Eve said

with a chuckle.

"I have," Scott agreed. "Which probably has something to do with how cryptic Adam was about it all."

"Yes, that was likely agitating." She pushed through the doors and revealed a massive room, far bigger than the rest of the spaces that they had seen combined. Bright white lights shone from the ceiling, presenting gargantuanly complicated steel structures to them. "I present to you, the Exodus Project's Dominion of Life," she said dramatically.

Scott drew in a quick breath. It was amazing. They were more detailed, beautiful, and precise than any design he had ever seen in his entire life. The things that he was looking at were exactly what he imagined when he thought of what could realistically be futuristic technology.

"What are they?"

"These are the ships that will be carrying humanity's last seeds of survival. They will take you to Jupiter, where you will either push us to grow into a new civilization or die."

Scott grinned uncontrollably. "We're going to space?" His voice was filled with a hope that he hadn't heard or thought of since he had been in elementary, or perhaps middle school. It had been the last time he had truly considered it possible to go to space.

"Yes, you are," Eve said with a short nod.

A thought struck him. "Are staff not invited?"

Eve shook her head. "It was that obvious?"

Scott shrugged. "You just didn't seem like you were excited."

"Regardless, I doubt most people would be excited after hearing the rest of it."

Scott tilted his head. "Why not?"

"Only around 5,000 people were picked for the Exodus Project. That means that all of your friends, family, hopes, and dreams, will be left on Earth. The rest of your life will be devoted to keeping humanity alive even just one fraction of a second longer. In essence, you must lose all that you love to become a slave. And for what? Is it even worth it?"

Scott watched the ships, wondering what each part did. Would she be able to tell him, or would he have to learn some other way? He couldn't wait to board and leave. There was just too much to learn for him not to feel that way.

"We have a very different mindset," he said at last after realizing that some time had passed without there having been a word said. "You believe leaving Earth to be a loss, and to that, I say that you are right. We are losing a great many things, and for people like you, things that are loved are among them. For me, however, there is little left that I love except for my own life and my curiosity. I have been granted the opportunity of a lifetime. I will not complain. I will learn as much as I can and die, full of love, as I will have fulfilled one of my only dreams that I had truly abandoned before stepping into this room."

"And what is that?"

"That I might one day go to space."

-9-

Scott felt oddly comfortable in the spacesuit. He remembered that in the training a lot of his peers had struggled with claustrophobia and the fact that they couldn't touch their faces, but he had not been among this group. He had always loved the way it hugged his body, almost as if it were telling him that it would always be there for him, even if his peers weren't.

Protocol required them to only allow one person out at a time on a spacewalk like that, and for whatever reason, Norgaard wouldn't allow for any deviations from it. They had wanted a maintenance worker to be the one to wear it, but Scott hadn't allowed it. He supposed he could have justified his actions with some sort of noble speech, however that would have been disingenuous. In truth, he just wanted to be in space. Something about the idea of stepping into the abyss was incredibly enticing to him. Nobody questioned him, though, and his justifications remained silent.

In his mind, he saw images of men in white suits floating through the void. Fictional depictions had always felt so peaceful. He approached the airlock that marked the edge of the ship and felt dread creeping into his heart. *This might be the end*, he thought, *but at least this is a good way to go.*

"The tether is secure," Scott heard in his ear.

"And the airlock has been evacuated."

He took a deep breath. "I stand upon the precipice of death. I do these things, not because they are noble, but because they bring me joy. Perhaps my purpose is impure and I will fall into the depths of hell. Or perhaps I will live and achieve greatness." He wasn't sure where the words had come from, just that they felt right.

With that, the doors into the void opened and Scott stepped out, falling into darkness, enveloped by pervasive nothingness. It wasn't nearly as silent and immobile as the spacewalks that he had heard of before. He was being pulled down, and with that came a strange fear of heights and the question of where he would go if the tether became detached. Of course, he knew the answer to that question, but he didn't believe in the truth behind it. His fear was too strong.

All he had to do was descend to the bottom of the ship, avoid getting burned by the other engines, and press a button that granted the engine the ability to be fully operated by the computer within. How the engine had even been turned off, he wasn't aware and was instead attempting to focus on his duty. Unfortunately, he couldn't shake the question of how it had happened out of his mind, and he found that his attention was being pulled in multiple directions.

Scott spun slowly as he descended. The accretion disk of the black hole was visible, if only barely. Everything was so dark. So impossibly dark. It felt like he was falling into a truly endless pit of despair. The vastness of space was too much, and before he had even reached the bottom of the vessel, Scott started to hyperventilate with panic.

And then a red light came into view. *Finally*, he thought. He reached to press the button but hesitated. What if there was a reason it had been closed? What if humanity wasn't supposed to live on? What if, by pressing that button, Scott would be subjecting his peers to damnation? He wouldn't be able to live with himself if that were the case.

"Are you safe?" a voice asked him. "Can you reach the button?"

"Yes."

Did he have a moral obligation to do so? Perhaps it wasn't so bad to be left behind. Perhaps fighting against the tide of nature was inherently bad. In those moments in the abyss, he felt more alone and lost than ever before. What was happening to him?

"Have you pressed it yet?"

"Not yet."

Their window was closing. Without proper adjustment, which would require fuel usage that they didn't have, they wouldn't be able to make it to Jupiter if he didn't act soon. He could feel the weight of the decision pushing down on him. It shouldn't have been affecting him as much as it was, yet it was all the same.

But how could he live with himself if he were to not press it? Whether or not they survived, if he were to return to the top without having pressed it, he would never be able to forgive himself. The world was cruel, or no, he was, for giving himself that choice. In that moment, he understood that humans were ill-equipped to handle the tasks of gods.

He closed his eyes and forced himself to clear his mind of all doubt. The button had to be pressed. Humanity had to endure. Scott felt ashamed that there had been even an ounce of conflict in his mind. The world had died, but they had not. They had lived. And he would only help them move on to better things.

He felt the button click below his hand and with it, some, but not all, of his shame vanished.

-10-

Scott stared at the wall as the timer on his bedside table counted down. There were only 1,567 seconds until departure. His hands trembled in his lap. The fear of death that had been placated by hope was returning with a vengeance. In his mind, dread fought against optimism, and it was winning.

He took his new phone out of his pocket and scrolled through the photo album that he had saved to the cloud. Tears formed in his eyes. He wished that he could have one more conversation with them. It had been so long ago and their time had been cut too short. He hated how all of the good things in life seemed to vanish just as quickly as they arrived.

Why did they have to leave? Why couldn't they have been with him during this next step in his life? He needed them then more than ever. The laughter of Sarah, the wisdom of Nairobi, and the calmness that always seemed to fall upon a room once Asa entered. All of his friends had died, though, falling and joining his family. They had all left him. So there he stood, the bringer of light to the future. The carrier of their hopes and dreams. In a sense he was the Atlas to their world, preventing it from collapsing in on itself and falling to pieces. The pressure was horrifyingly monstrous, yet he loved it all the same.

He set his phone down and wiped the wetness from his face. It was no time to cry. His dreams were about to come true. The infinity of space would soon be his home. He had imagined that moment since he had first seen space in fiction, and ever since then, his life had been completely changed.

An alarm dinged as the timer hit 1,500 seconds, signaling to him that it was time to go. Scott stared at his bags before grabbing them. Had his entire life been reduced to the size of a few, not even fully filled, duffle bags?

Unsure of how to feel by that, he slung them over his shoulder and then stepped into the hall where a janitor was cleaning. He looked unfamiliar, but that wasn't unusual with much of the maintenance crew around Kytos. Most of them remained in the shadows, trying as best as they could to stay out of the way.

Something about this man unnerved Scott even more than just the fact that he had never seen him before. Scott couldn't place why, but the man felt dangerous, almost like he was threatening something. The hairs on the back of his neck pricked up as he walked by.

Down the hall he went, truly attempting to ignore those horrid feelings and the effects that they had had on him. He wanted to instead focus on how great things were about to become.

He fell into place in line to his ship, Number 13. Number 13 was unremarkable, completely identical to all of the other of the hundreds of ships going. However, since Scott was one of the people on the ship, he had elected to think of it as the best one for no other reason than because he felt like it.

The line eased into the vessel as the time counted down. They had drilled this exact scenario enough before for Scott to know that they were being as efficient as possible. The people boarding needed to be able to get to their rooms without hindrance and loading too many people at once would inhibit their progress. It felt like it was taking forever, but it would soon be over, and they would be on their way.

At last, it was Scott's turn to board. He immediately rushed to his room, taking care not to fall or collide with anything, and unpacked once he had arrived. There, he strapped himself to his bed where he would have to stay until the launch stage of the mission had concluded.

His mind whirled with thoughts of excitement and pessimism. What if he became an incredible historic figure? What if instead, Number 34 was destroyed during launch? There were so many possibilities, and Scott felt as if time was granting him the ability to consider all of them.

Without warning, he felt gravity increase as the ground shook beneath his back. They were launching already. Scott couldn't believe how exhilarating it felt. They were leaving Earth behind in exchange for life.

Those who stayed behind would live, but only for a few days longer. Soon, the world would become far too cold for survivability and the last of humanity on Earth would freeze. There were those who were wealthy enough to design cryogenic pods with hopes of revival at a later date or those who had committed suicide so that they could control their fate, and none of them had ever known about the Exodus Project and the hope that it brought.

As they rose, the sun would be undergoing its final reactions, being extinguished by some force that scientists were still too incompetent to understand. They had planned for the mission to leave exactly as that happened to give themselves as much time as possible to prepare. It was insane to Scott just how close they had cut it.

In the midst of all of these ideas, something clicked in Scott's mind. His earlier discomfort was no longer quite so strange. Why had the janitor been cleaning if he was aware that the world was about to end?

-11-

The culprit hated everything about the Exodus Project. It was horrifyingly sacrilegious, completely abandoning all morality for an unnaturally long life. To leave Earth is to abandon all that is holy. Never would he have thought to do something like that for his own, personal gain. And now they had gone and forced him to come along. He hoped that he would be able to stop them before too much damage had been done.

He had been blessed by their ignorance when formulating his noble plot. He supposed that he had likely been blessed by the heavens as well, seeing as they had been the ones to grant him the opportunities that he had taken advantage of. Without the help of the divine, he wouldn't have worked for the government and gotten a job at Kytos only to help design, or rather interfere with the design, of the Exodus Project.

There was so much at play with his plans that he himself was beginning to feel like a pawn in them. It was hard to keep track of everything, and he frequently had to remind himself that whatever he was doing was the right thing as he had been chosen by the heavens.

It was easy enough to sabotage, that much had already become clear, but only a few of the ships had been hit by his attacks. The rest of them were completely fine, being sent to Jupiter where they would connect to form the living hell that humanity sought to call home. They were all fools.

If he wanted to make real change, though, and deliver his race to the grave that had already been dug for it, he needed more than just cheap tricks and his wit. He needed a following who believed in his cause. He needed an uprising. And more than anything, he needed an event that would show humanity how egregious its errors were. People had to know how necessary voluntary suicide was, and nothing short of a miracle would give him the results he desired.

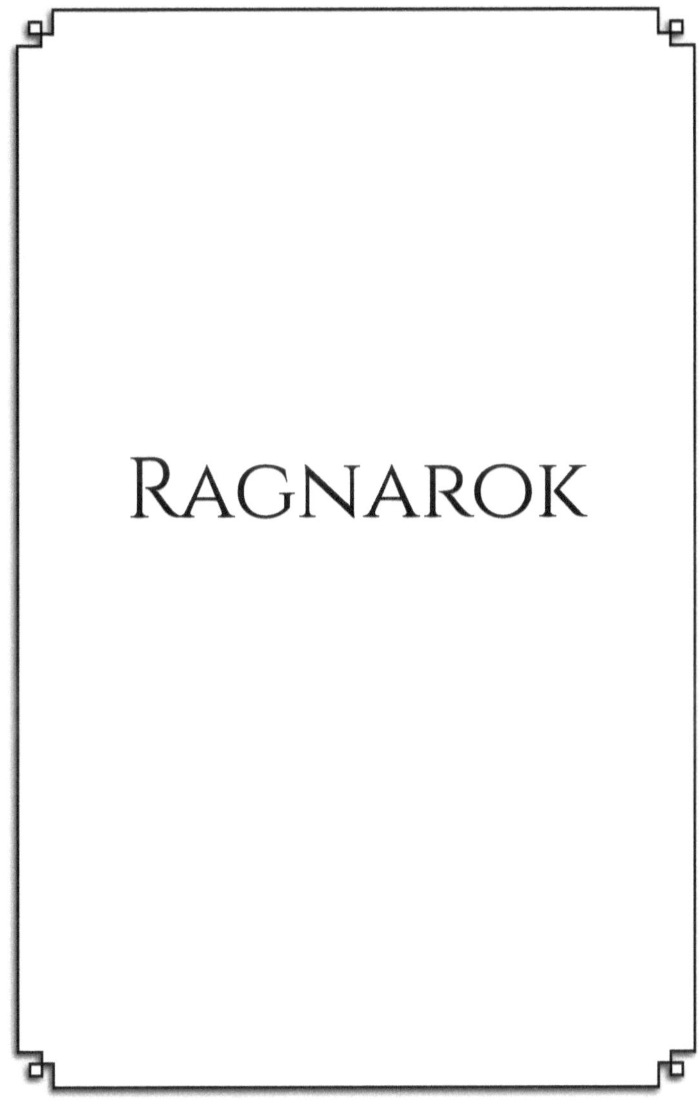

Ragnarok

-1-

Juliette wandered through the rainforest, completely entranced by its beauty. From the way she looked upon it, an outside observer would have assumed that this was her first time visiting the conservatory. This, of course, wasn't true. She had visited the rainforest almost every day since she had discovered it as a young girl, but that didn't take any of the magic away from it.

Frogs croaked in harmony with the white noise that the various insect species produced. Water dripped from damp leaves through which rays of artificial sunlight shone. The skydome high above looked real enough, but Juliette supposed that she had nothing to compare it to. She had never seen a true blue sky on Earth. She had never even been to Earth, for that matter. It had ended long before she was born, leaving humanity to live aboard *the Dominion of Life*.

She brushed her hand across a cacao leaf, getting some of its moisture on her in the process. A lizard climbed up one of the trees to her left, barely catching her eye. There was so much to focus on, so much to see, to hear, to smell, to experience, that she couldn't help but feel slightly overwhelmed. Yet, that was what she loved most.

The rest of the station, aside from the few genuinely interesting conversations she had with her friends and family, was painfully boring. Outside the conservatory, there were only workplaces and residential areas, which were both composed mostly of metal and glass, showing the depressingly dark void of space at all times.

Feeling herself growing frustrated, Juliette shifted her focus from her life to the log that she had to balance on to get across the creek below it. She wobbled slightly as she wasn't very coordinated even after all of the time that she had spent in the jungle, and leaped across to the other side when it got close enough. Her feet sank slightly into the mud, dirtying her shoes even more than they had already been.

Something interesting caught her eye. A plant she had never seen before was sitting in front of her. Or wait. She got closer and saw that it wasn't a plant but rather a fungus. There were dark brown and gray spots covering the ground, appearing to be some sort of disease. It was terrifying and new, and interestingly enough, Juliette found that she even liked it.

18 O'CLOCK, the intercom screamed, interrupting her peace. *Jacques will be getting home soon*, she thought with a resigned sigh. It seemed that no matter how much she wished to use the rainforest as an escape, there were always things that would reach out to tear her from the immersion.

Hesitantly, as she did not want to leave the fungus, she navigated her way back to the exit, taking the time to use one of the washing stations provided. She hosed off her muddy shoes, checked herself for any other signs of grime, and reluctantly pushed herself to finally leave the conservatory.

Every time she left, it felt like there was a magnet pulling her back, begging her not to have left in the first place, and every time, Juliette had to get just a bit stronger to ignore it. She knew that there would likely be a time when she would never want to leave the rainforest and wondered what she would do when that time came. How soon would it come, for that matter? Very soon, if nothing in her life changed shortly.

Her husband, Jacques, had never done anything to make her feel loved or wanted, so she had never desired to be in his company. It was a simple thing to Juliette, of which she didn't think much about, but strangely to those close to her, this was horrific. They often spoke of marriage as if it were supposed to be a union on the basis of love, but Juliette thought that that was an archaic concept. Perhaps during the times of Old Earth, when there were more people, that made sense. Now, marriage was cold and statistical, meant for keeping humanity alive.

But it wasn't that Juliette hated her husband. No, that certainly wasn't it. It was just that when she thought of him, she found that she felt nothing, and conversely, she loved the rainforest. So if she had to pick between the two, the choice was obvious.

Instinctively, she checked the control panel on her way out. As a maintenance worker, the government had done well to condition her into doing her job, even when she was supposedly on break. She scrolled through the menus, checking to make sure that nothing was wrong. The reactor was at 90% efficiency, the air was clean, and the acceleration value was 9.8, which she had learned was their target. Everything seemed to be mostly in order.

The cold metal casing of dominion swallowed her, echoing hollowly as she walked through the corridor. They said that it was full of life, but to Juliette, the station was the most dead thing she could think of.

The lights above were no longer as natural and beautiful as could be found in the conservatory, and at eye level, instead of leaves and animals, there were holes in the walls. They appeared to be an odd design choice, and she had no understanding of why they had been added. To her, it had always felt like someone was watching through the holes as she walked.

A guard passed by, presumably on patrol, and Juliette waved, attempting to be friendly even though she had never met the man. He tapped the side of his head and then glared at her. She frowned, unsure of what she had done to earn outright disdain from him. He passed by without a word. She couldn't help but feel on edge, as if she had done something wrong.

Moments later, the echo of footsteps on metal faded only to be replaced by a thunderous stampeding. Juliette frantically searched around, hoping to see where the danger was coming from and was soon met by a wave of guards. They sprinted past her, shouting incomprehensibly, although she was fairly certain that she had heard one or two of them mention an explosion.

She froze where she was standing, wondering what the best thing to do might be. If she followed, she might be able to learn more about whatever was causing them so much anxiety, and maybe she could relax. However, she knew that she would just get in the way and maybe even get herself in trouble, so she continued walking as she had been before.

The hallway stopped at a t-intersection. Juliette went right as she always did and for no real reason other than the fact that she was listening to an impulse, she looked left. Down the hall, shrouded in a shadow so dark that she could hardly see, was a man. She wasn't sure how she knew, but she could tell that he was wrong. What that meant, she didn't know; it was just a feeling.

Without any warning, the man retreated further into the darkness, leaving Juliette staring at nothing but shadow. How odd. She kept walking and headed home to meet Jacques before he arrived. As she went, she couldn't quite help but to wonder who that had been and whether or not she should report it. At her doorstep, she decided that she wouldn't say anything. They probably wouldn't have listened anyway.

To call her humble abode a house was a massive overstatement. It was a collection of metal rooms built into the wall of the residential area, using space as efficiently as possible. At least, that was according to the government. It seemed to her that they thought tiny and efficient were synonyms. She hardly had enough room to get comfortable by herself, let alone with Jacques. Not for the first time that day, she was grateful that her husband was an inner system explorer. He was hardly ever home. To prevent him from taking his aggression out on her while they were together, she made an effort to make him happy. She hated how disingenuous she had to be at times.

She triple-checked each room to make sure that they had been fully cleaned. Sure enough, they had been. She knew that but was still nervous she had made a mistake along the way and forgotten something. The kitchen smelled of roast beef, his favorite, and the timer told her that it would be done soon, hopefully in time for his return.

Twiddling her thumbs anxiously, Juliette wondered, for the dozenth time since she had returned home if she had time to run and talk to her family. That had always helped to calm her nerves. But no. Just as she was about to get up and go, the door clicked open, and Jacques walked through.

Young, athletic, tall, cold Jacques, who had never given her anything but indifference.

"Welcome home," she said monotonously. "Roast beef is in the oven and should be done soon."

He grunted, not meeting her gaze as he went and dropped his things into their room. Juliette felt a pit of frustration open in her gut, which only grew when she tried to remind herself that she shouldn't care. She had done so much work for him, though, and not to receive even a single word of greeting or thanks was just rude.

She heard him clanging around in the other room and went to see what he was doing. In their tiny bathroom, he stood. He took off his over-garments to reveal a blood-stained undershirt. Any normal wife would have panicked and rushed to her husband's side, and Juliette hated the fact that she wished that was what she and Jacques had. However, she resolved to stay where she was and silently watch.

Jacques peeked over at her with a look of contempt that almost seemed to say, "Why are you here?" Instead, all he said was, "Hey."

"Hey," Juliette replied coolly. She was not going to ask what happened.

"It's dangerous out there," he explained, turning his attention back to the wound. "Things get out of hand, and people get hurt."

"I see that."

He peeled off his undershirt and blood immediately started to flow down his pants. It seemed that the shirt had done something to stop the bleeding and tearing it off so haphazardly had only reopened the wound. She couldn't tell because of the redness, but it looked like the wound was a cut that was about 3 or 4 inches long. It looked to be quite deep based on the amount of blood, and she assumed that medical attention was necessary, but she would not recommend that to him. He was an adult, too, and knew how to make his own decisions.

Tired of wasting her time with him, Juliette returned to the kitchen to wait for the beef to be done. She checked the oven timer. **0:56**, it read. Maybe getting him some food would put him in a better mood. She stood in the kitchen, unsure if she was excited or nervous for it to finish cooking. At last, a ding sounded and Juliette put on her oven mitts and pulled the beef out.

She set it on a dish that she had prepared for it and then checked on the gravy, which was staying warm by the heat of the stove. *Should I get the dishes out for him?* The thought was brief, and she came to a swift, decisive no.

Jacques strode back into the kitchen a few moments later, wearing a new shirt. Other than that change, he appeared to be in near perfect condition, and if Juliette hadn't seen his wound, she would have assumed that that was how he felt as well.

Without a word, she placed the entire roast beef and the whole pot of gravy in front of him. He went and grabbed silverware out of the cabinet and greedily dug in, staying silent.

Juliette's anger grew beyond her control. "That's it? I make you a nice meal and this is how you treat me? No 'thank you,' or even 'this looks delicious?!'" She felt her breath drawing short. "You are always so unbelievably rude."

Calmly, Jacques set his knife down on the table. "You know my feelings towards you," he said. "You weren't even my third choice."

Juliette swallowed hard. Her eyes burned with hatred that she thought she had suppressed.

"I don't hate you, nor do I feel any malevolence towards you. Instead, I pity myself that I got stuck with you and wonder if life could have been different if I would have been able to learn about love. Instead, I got stuck with you. I don't hate or seethe; I simply wish that things would have been different."

Juliette grabbed her coat from where she had so perfectly draped it over the tiny chair that she liked to call their couch.

"I hope you take solace in the fact that I have never hated you. I am only this cold around you because you are not the one for me and I know I could never possibly feel any sort of love towards you."

With that, he put the tip of the knife and fork on the roast and started to cut eagerly. Softly crying, Juliette could see that what he was saying was true. He cared more about the meal than he had ever cared about her. Unable to contain herself, she whipped around and ran through their front door.

-2-

Ebuka Abdullahi had never been known for her compassion. Those who knew her had always said that she was heartless, valuing numbers over people, but those who knew her well knew that instead she had a passion for the statistics of life. She had always thought of math as beauty, almost even an art. It controlled the universe in ways that she could hardly begin to imagine, and from a young age she figured out that her time would be best spent studying it.

Unfortunately for the idealism of a child, the real world was far less organized and simple than she would have liked. Problems came about that interrupted the order of things, complicating the math that described reality. It infuriated her to no end, and it got to the point that she figured she might as well take a crack at stopping discord in the first place, leading her to become a member of *the Dominion* Congress.

The moment she had been elected by her community, she had known that that was where she belonged. The strategy, the intrigue, the planning, and corruption, all of it inspired her to make the changes that she knew would make *the Dominion of Life* the best place it could be.

Her assistant appeared by her side with a cup of coffee. Without acknowledging him, she took it and continued to work on her tablet. They had a sort of mutual understanding that Ebuka did care for him, as she cared for all people, and found that taking the time to prove it each day was rather exhausting.

"Congressman Tanaka would like to speak to you about a bill concerning disease prevention and another related to crime rates," he started. Ebuka would have preferred that he stay silent, as she was quite immersed in her work, but she wouldn't say anything. He was just doing his job. "He says that it is important."

"They always say these things are important, Tim," she replied with a slight bite to her tone. "Would you say that it is worth my time, truly?"

"After having skimmed over it," Tim began as he always did even though he was the type to thoroughly read everything handed to him, "I believe that it would be a 6 on the Abdullahi Scale."

Ebuka was very grateful for the Abdullahi Scale. It had streamlined communications and provided her with an easy way to determine urgency when dealing with threats. A 10 referred to a problem that required her immediate attention, a 1 was something she could ignore, and it had never failed her.

"Violent crime is up 4% this year," she thought aloud. "The Japanese community has no connections to it, or at least they haven't seen as much of the impact from the attacks as of late, which could be why Tanaka is pushing this right now."

"Perhaps he feels that boosting public health would look good on both of your records," Tim proposed.

"Perhaps. However, the timing is rather odd. There hasn't been a significant rise in disease-related deaths as of late, at least not that I have seen."

"The Japanese disease-related death rate increased by 2% last year," Tim added.

"I'm going to say that we say no to this one," Ebuka said as she shook her head. "The timing is suspect at best, and there already isn't enough money going to the police. I just don't see where we could reasonably make cuts."

Tim nodded in her periphery and then disappeared, leaving her to continue her work. It felt good to finally be alone, with both her thoughts and her work. Even just having someone else in the room made it harder for her to think.

She quickly became absorbed in her bill, which proposed an increase in defense spending to reduce the rising crime rates. She had always been a strong proponent of having a powerful defense force, especially because of the relative instability of the station, however, not all of her peers felt the same way.

There was so much opposition, in fact, that of the 342 bills that she had proposed during her thirty-some years in Congress, she had passed 0. Not a single one had been appealing enough to earn a majority vote.

Even so, she persevered still, knowing that her work would someday benefit *the Dominion*. With her efforts, an agent of discord could be defeated.

17 O'CLOCK, the robotic voice of the clock shrieked. Ebuka cringed. Perhaps she should have been working on a bill to propose a more relaxed voice for the intercom. She knew why it had been so ear-splitting, remembering a discussion about how it was more likely to wake up the required maintenance workers on time, but still, she hated it with every ounce of her being.

"I need to leave a bit early today," Ebuka shouted to Tim as she stood up from her desk. Usually, they left at 18, but that day was an exception.

"A meeting?" he asked, not looking up from his tablet.

"An experiment," she replied. "I need to go check my data."

"Enjoy," he said with a knowing smile. Ebuka could see something behind his eyes, something foreign that she would not ask about. His eyes were bright, carrying darkness, however at the same time they told her to look elsewhere, and she found it strange that she trusted them.

The tiny box that Ebuka watched from wasn't as constrictive as people, more specifically Tim, made it seem. Yes, her shoulders were squeezed between two walls and she had just enough space to fully breathe in without her chest touching the wall in front of her, but that didn't mean that it was too small. In her eyes, there was still space that could have been removed, and for that reason, it was even too big.

People walked by and she watched, recording their behaviors and feelings with nothing but her mind. He is unhappy. She wishes that she wouldn't have to be a maintenance worker. His side is bothering him, were all thoughts that passed through her head as she stood and observed, collecting the necessary data to make real change.

She knew that some people might call her observations weird, creepy even, but she didn't care. It was the best way to watch them. The station didn't allow for the use of security cameras due to recent privacy laws that had been pushed by the Swiss community, and she was far too introverted to feel the need to talk to people about how they felt. On top of that, she was almost certain that if she were to ask questions or to try to get to know the people, they would feel extremely uncomfortable due to her station and not answer with complete honesty. At least with that method, she got true results.

18 O'CLOCK, the intercom echoed through the hallway, getting a slight jump out of Ebuka. Her limbs clanged and banged against the metal walls as she tried to regain her bearings. It was one of the most uncomfortable situations that she had ever experienced. Pain covered her body like a thin blanket. She hoped that no one had heard her. Part of the strength behind her data collection was that no one knew she was watching.

A few moments later, a short and stocky French woman walked by. From what Ebuka could tell, she looked sad, almost even hateful. Ebuka pitied the woman, wishing there was something she could do to directly help.

Shortly after, a guard passed by with a panicked look on his face. Ebuka immediately forced every bit of her attention onto him, hoping that with a glance she would be able to understand what was happening. Normal people interested her, but guards were something else entirely, relating directly to the prevention of the discord that she despised so much.

Her brain filled with conflicting ideas as she struggled with whether or not she should get out and follow or if she should just watch. Then, he started to run, and Ebuka knew what she had to do. The box had served its purpose and provided her with something interesting, and now it was time to leave it behind and move on to the next steps of proper reconnaissance.

When she was certain that no one could see her step out of the wall, she pressed the exit button by her hip and deftly removed herself from her hiding spot. For a second or two she looked around, feeling her hair standing on edge as if she was being watched. Had someone seen her? No, that's just paranoia, she reassured herself.

A group of guards blew past her, following after the first one she had seen. So something had happened, then. Ebuka stifled a curious smile. If the guards were that worried about it, it was likely serious.

Ahead of her, they turned a corner. When she arrived at the intersection of the halls, she found that she had no idea which way they had gone. All three passages were empty. Feeling frustration rising in her chest, she began to think of ways to determine the best way to find out which way they had gone. Someone bumped into her from the back.

She whipped around to see who it might be, on edge after having seen the guards. She let out a relieved breath after seeing that it was only Tim.

"What are *you* doing here?" she asked.

"I saw some guards running that way," he said, pointing

down one of the empty halls. "So I ran the other way. What are you doing here?"

Ebuka laughed. She liked her assistant, but sometimes their differences were painfully obvious. "I was collecting data when I saw some guards running, and decided that it would be in my best interest to follow."

Tim tilted his head and looked at her quizzically. "Sometimes I wonder if you are a Congresswoman or a journalist."

"To make real change, I suppose I must be a little bit of both," she replied, chuckling.

Tim clenched his jaw, looking ahead, to where Ebuka was headed and back to where he was originally running. "I don't suppose running would make me seem like a coward," he said.

"There would be no judgment from my end," Ebuka shrugged. "I do have to go, though. This window may soon close, and I would very much like to capitalize on the opportunity at hand."

With that, she turned and went down the hallway that Tim had told her to follow. A few seconds later, she heard the reluctant footsteps of her assistant and felt him at her side. "Shit," he muttered. "Why am I doing this?"

"Because you are of the rare breed that cares more about the truth than your own wellbeing."

"That makes me sound insane."

"That's because you are. All of us are," she said with a smile. "That's what makes this fun."

They walked in a silence that was surrounded by fear that Ebuka would never have admitted existed. Thoughts of what it could have been raced through her mind. What if there was a leak, or one of the reactors went offline? The results would have been catastrophic.

She felt her heartbeat quicken the further they went. The suspense was killing her. She needed to find out what had happened.

Suddenly, the lights started to flicker. The visibility was inconsistent, preventing Ebuka from being able to get reliable data about their surroundings. It almost looked like there were red stains on the ground. She wished the lighting would have been better so that she could have confirmed all suspicions she had about its origin.

The more she walked, the thicker the red stains got and the faster the flickers became. Her feet slipped on what she knew was blood. There was no use denying it now. People had died. A massacre. The lights went out, leaving them to stand in darkness, together but alone with their thoughts at the same time.

An instant later, the lights flashed on, and Ebuka gasped when she saw what had happened. Next to her, Tim puked. She couldn't blame him. It was easily the most gruesome thing she had ever seen. There were twelve heads on spikes, their eyes scratched out and their bodies strewn about below. Their guts had been brutally ripped from their chests. It looked more like an attack by a monster than a man. All of the guards that she had watched run had been murdered in cold blood.

And on the wall, written in blood, was one, foreboding word:

RAGNAROK

-3-

Juliette loved talking to her mother. She was the only person that Juliette felt that she could go to when she needed help. She had been there through everything, through every scrape and bruise to every heartbreak. It was nice to know that there was someone watching, caring for her.

"So tell me exactly what happened," Mother said while holding a sobbing Juliette. Her embrace was warm and comforting, relieving Juliette of her sorrows.

"Why does he have to be so cold?" Juliette cried.

"What did he do?"

Juliette opened her mouth to reply, but her words were interrupted by uncontrollable weeping. She hated that he had so much control over her to make her act like that. In times like those, she felt weak. There was no reason that he should have been able to hurt her so. She had already decided that she didn't care about him. But in truth, she knew that she did.

"It's okay, dear," her mom said, shushing her as she rubbed her back. "Let your sadness flow out of you with your tears until you can talk about your pain."

So Juliette cried in her mother's arms, the only arms that she knew she could always return to. She cried with pain, and she cried with gratitude. Her emotions flowed without hindrance, and Juliette found that she was glad for this fact. She felt like she was being her genuine self.

After some time, Juliette pushed herself from her mother's chest and wiped her nose. "You want to hear what happened?"

"Yes, please, tell me."

Juliette sniffled. "Well, Jacques was scheduled to come home today," she began.

"Oh honey," her mother said, leaning forward to grab Juliette's hand in her own. "Did you get your hopes up again? You know that he's not nearly as romantic as you'd like him to be."

"No, I know," Juliette said, shaking her head. "I'm not upset that he didn't run to me to give me love." She searched within herself and found that this was a lie. She was upset. She wished they had a relationship similar to the ones that she read about. "What I'm upset about is how blatantly rude he was to me."

"What did he do?"

"I made roast beef and gravy for him since I know that that's his favorite food," she began. "But then, when he got home, he didn't even acknowledge that I was there. I said 'hi' and everything, and he just ignored me and dropped his things off, and then went to the bathroom. From there, he took his shirt off and I saw a huge gash along his side. It was really bloody."

"Is he okay?" her mom asked.

"He didn't tell me otherwise," Juliette shrugged. "And why should I even care? He's an asshole."

"He might be rude, but he's still another life," her mother said.

Juliette clenched her jaw and nodded. Maybe during the times of old, when lives meant so much less, she could have said something like that and received support, but not anymore. Even the worst of society were considered assets for their reproductive abilities and contributions to a broader gene pool.

"Well, anyway. He cleaned himself up and came out to the kitchen where I had served him his dinner, and he didn't bother to say anything about it, choosing to start eating instead."

"How rude!"

"But that's not even the worst part!" Juliette exclaimed.

She heard footsteps. Moments later, Aunt Joan's head appeared around the corner. "What's not even the worst part?" she asked.

"Juliette was telling me about Jacques," her mother explained.

"What about that snake?"

"You didn't miss much," Juliette interjected. She could feel a slight smile forming on her face. It always felt good to be able to talk to her family when she had problems. They had an uncanny ability to cheer her up, even when the worst things had happened. "He came home from work and didn't say anything to me even after I made dinner for him."

"What an ass!" Aunt Joan yelled.

"Then, after I asked him why he felt the need to be so mean to me, he went on this long rant about how I was never right for him, and he pities himself for allowing himself to be married to me." Tears filled her eyes as she said these words. It hurt even with her family there to support her.

"Oh, honey," Aunt Joan said, rushing forward to hug her. "That's terrible. I'm so sorry."

And Suddenly Juliette was crying all over again. Why did she have to be so emotional, especially about someone who wasn't? It was exhausting. She wished that she could live in a cabin in the rainforests of Old Earth with her family, never needing to see Jacques again. God, that sounded like heaven.

It took her a moment to realize that her mother owned some of the arms that were hugging her as well, and they were not all just Joan's. She was grateful that they were there and so supportive. It was nice. She just wished that Jacques was anything like them. Her life would have been infinitely easier if that had been the case.

A knock came from the front door. Immediately, Juliette's heart leaped. What if it was an angry Jacques? What if he had come to take her home? The idea of it made her skin crawl.

"I'll get it," Joan said quickly, clearly able to see the nervousness plastered across her niece's face.

Before her aunt had even opened the door, Juliette had already decided that she wouldn't go. What would he do? Try to take her by force? No, that wasn't like him. But if he were to try to, Joan and Mother were there, and there were guards nearby. She would be okay.

"Hello." she heard. That didn't sound like Jacques. "My name is Ebuka Abdullahi." And that wasn't Jacques's name either. "This is my associate, Timothy Drummond. Would it be alright if we asked a Juliette Lavigne about an event that transpired earlier today?"

Joan turned around and looked to Juliette for her approval. "What's up?" Juliette asked, beckoning for them to come in. One of them was an older woman with darker skin, likely from the Nigerian Sector, and the other was clearly of European descent, although Juliette couldn't place from where specifically. The woman joined Juliette and her mother at the table while the man stood next to Joan in the hall that led to the front door.

"What do you remember about what you saw of the guards when you were walking in the halls no more than an hour ago?"

Juliette tilted her head, trying to recall exactly what. "They seemed spooked like something was wrong. It was weird, though, because at first, I thought that one of them was glaring at me and thinking of me as a target."

"Did a group of guards run past you?"

"Yes."

"Did you hear them say anything in passing?"

Juliette frowned. "Not that I can remember. Most of it was just incomprehensible shouting. Why do you ask?"

The woman's expression changed from inquisitive to stern, almost as if she had changed masks at a moment's notice. "Because moments after seeing you, these twelve men were brutally murdered, ripped to pieces, their heads placed upon pikes, with the word 'Ragnarok' written on the wall behind them in blood."

Juliette's eyes widened. "What?"

"Unfortunately, this ship is not home to quite as many peaceful people as we in Congress would like to believe."

"What are you going to do about this?" Mother asked. "That's horrible. Who is going to replace the guards? How will their families be compensated? How are you going to find who did this?"

The questions fell out of her mother's mouth like a rainstorm, and Ebuka never once interrupted her to tell her that she needed to calm down. Instead, the woman, who Juliette had just learned was a Congresswoman, listened to all of Mother's frustrations and concerns. It was refreshing and sweet to see, and Juliette found that seeing her mom being cared for made her feel better about the fact that she had just learned about a massacre. Suddenly her qualms with Jacques felt insubstantial.

"Those are all brilliantly astute questions," Ebuka said after Mother was done. "In time, we will have all of the answers that you desire. However, as this has just happened, I am afraid that you and I carry the same amount of ignorance on what is going to happen."

"Tell me you at least have a plan," Joan cut in.

Ebuka turned and looked at Timothy with a raised eyebrow. "I am currently working on drafting letters to other representatives regarding this event. Hopefully, with the support of Congress, we will be able to prevent this from happening again."

"And this was in the French Sector?" Juliette asked.

"Yes," Ebuka replied.

"Why isn't Congressman Petain doing anything about it then? Why are you here instead?"

Ebuka shrugged. "I was in the neighborhood, and I imagine that if he has heard the news, it has been only recently."

"What does Ragnarok mean?" Juliette asked. "As in what is the significance of that word in relation to the crime?"

Ebuka smiled.

"What's entertaining?" Mother asked, immediately jumping in as if she needed to take Juliette's side.

"I apologize if you thought I was amused by your question," Ebuka said, bowing respectfully to Juliette. "I was only smiling because I am impressed by the level of thinking that you are applying to this situation. You are all asking the right questions, and it's honestly extremely impressive."

Juliette sat up a little straighter at the sound of these words. Praise from a congresswoman was surely quite a rare thing.

"And now, to answer your question, Ragnarok is, in simple terms, Norse mythology's representation of the end of the world. It is when the gods are killed, the heavens are plunged into darkness, and the universe is reduced to ash."

"Is someone trying to say that they will destroy *the Dominion of Life?*" Juliette asked softly. The idea terrified her. She didn't want to die.

"It seems likely," Ebuka admitted. "There are an incredible amount of parallels with the most notable one being the floating city of Asgard and the fact that our home is essentially a floating island."

"The implications behind this are scary," Timothy said with a short nod.

"Does the French Sector have enough guards after this?" Joan asked. "Are we safe?"

"Likely not, although it isn't a big deal. There are contingencies for scenarios such as these, and the other sectors will provide the French with some of their reserves." This news appeared to placate Joan, if only slightly. "I would like to assure you all, though, that this station is still a safe place for you to live. Even with this threat on board, you needn't live in fear. The monarch will handle this quickly and efficiently, and Congress will only help. After all, your safety is our priority. So much death isn't ideal, to say the least."

"We thank you for keeping us informed," Mother said. "Is there anything else you would like to ask? Would you like anything to eat, or drink while you are here?"

"No, but thank you. We really must be getting on our way. I appreciate your hospitality, though. You three have been exceptionally kind and accommodating."

With that, Ebuka rose from where she was seated at the table, and with Timothy, she retreated to the doorway. Juliette let out a breath that she didn't realize that she had been holding. "What has the world come to?" Mother asked with fear in her eyes. "We almost all died when the sun went out, and we're still fighting? This is absolutely ridiculous."

"It seems that no matter the catastrophe, human nature cannot be changed," Ebuka replied as she paused in the threshold.

"Which is?"

"Humans ride a line between life and death every day. In the middle, there is the conflict of the survivors. It appears that death will always have immense power over us, affecting even the way we act before it."

This seemed to satisfy Mother, for no further questions were asked. The congresswoman and her associate left without speaking any longer, except for a quick 'goodbye' from Timothy. Before Juliette's family knew it, though, they were alone again, now with an entirely new, and scary perception of the world.

-4-

Ebuka stretched out her hips as they stood outside of Juliette's mother's house. With age, they had begun to tighten up when she walked for extended periods, and it seemed that she was nearing her limit already. How frustrating. Perhaps she could get Tim to carry her.

"I think that went quite well," Tim said.

"In terms of how diplomatic we were, then I suppose it did. However, we didn't learn anything other than the fact that the people are just as ignorant as we are."

"Yes, I guess you're right. But that's not the worst thing ever, is it?"

"How can we expect to catch a criminal that is hidden even from the community within which it operates?" Ebuka asked, her voice stern now.

Tim shook his head and shrugged.

"Luckily, we don't have enough data to say that they are truly hidden from their community. We just know that Juliette Lavigne and her family are unaware of the truth, and they are only three. We inevitably will find someone who can give us some information, especially with such a high-profile case."

"That makes sense," Tim replied. "What are our next steps, then?"

"I think the monarch would enjoy a visit from us," Ebuka said with a wolfish smile. "The two of us have not talked in quite some time."

"Is that a good idea?"

"Why wouldn't it be?"

"The two of you have a rather complicated relationship, wouldn't you say?"

"I would," Ebuka replied, smiling. "That's what makes it so fun."

Monarch Norgaard stared at Ebuka with icy eyes. That was to be expected. What was unexpected, however, was the small terrarium that was sitting between the two of them. Inside, a lizard consumed a small, unidentifiable rodent. At first, Ebuka had been unsure if the monarch's gaze had been reserved for the rodent or her but then their eyes locked and all doubt fled her mind.

"It is fantastic to see you," Tim said from behind Ebuka, likely trying to relieve some of the tension in the room.

"Shhhhhh!" Ebuka said to him. "He was lying. It is awful to see you," she continued, turning toward the monarch.

"Why have you come?" the monarch asked, her tone just as cold as her expression.

"Because of the recent events in the French Sector," Ebuka replied.

"The guard is handling them," the monarch said dismissively. She was old. Too old to be in charge of anything important. Ebuka wished Congress could vote her out, but no matter how hard they tried, she stuck around. It was infuriating. She hadn't done anything in years except judge those she believed to be below her, which was everyone.

"The guard has been massacred," Ebuka replied calmly. "If I had to guess, which I don't, I would say that they are scrambling to fix their current issues surrounding being short-staffed."

"It's good that they can handle their own problems," the monarch grumbled sarcastically.

Ebuka stopped herself before she could roll her eyes. Just a second ago, the monarch seemed ready to give the guard all of the agency, and now she was acting like they never did anything. Which was it?

"I came to you because I think it's clear that they can't," Ebuka responded. "Twelve of them were killed brutally, made into symbols for the beginnings of a movement called Ragnarok. I am imploring you to help with whatever resources you have available."

The monarch's lips drew to a line. "You wish to use me, then."

Ebuka almost scoffed. How had she come to that conclusion? She sounded insane. "I wish for you to fulfill your duty to the people."

Monarch Norgaard shook her ancient head. "My duty to the people in your eyes is to resign from my position. Your distorted view of this world will be your downfall, but it will not be mine."

Ebuka took a deep, calming breath. Talking to the older woman was impossible because of their history. *Why did I even think to come to her?* Ebuka thought. She could have easily guessed that nothing productive was going to come out of one of their meetings.

Frustrated and no longer willing to restrain herself, Ebuka dropped all of the masks she was wearing. "You're right," she snapped. "I do want you to fall. But that is not because I hate you. I don't. I pity you. I think that you have forsaken your people for power, and it is disgusting, but I do not hate you. You are weak, and because of that, you should resign and let somebody else take over as monarch."

The monarch's eyes burned with rage, and Ebuka felt just a hint of satisfaction. She loved that she had enough control over the older woman that she could sway her mood with just a few words. It was strangely empowering.

Norgaard opened her mouth to speak, but Ebuka interrupted her before she could begin. "I must be on my way now. There are things I must attend to that will actually benefit the people. If you change your mind and become useful, though, feel free to contact me. I can give you some pointers on how to solve problems."

Abruptly, she got up from where she was seated and left with Tim. There was no reason to stay and talk any longer; the result would be the same as if they hadn't even had a meeting in the first place.

"So that's it?" Tim asked in the hall. "You plan to antagonize the figurehead of the human race? What if she tries to have you killed? Or worse?"

Ebuka turned and looked at Tim with a grin. "If she has the resources to have me killed, then she has the resources to stop this Ragnarok business. So part of me wants her to at least try. Maybe then we will be able to affect change."

The general attitude of the guard was not sad, nor was it quiet; it was angry. Ebuka wasn't surprised by this, although she was interested to find that Tim was. Who wouldn't be furious when their friends were killed? It seemed like such a simple connection to her.

The police station, or the guard station as some people called it, was orderly and clean, although Ebuka could see that quite a few things were not as organized as they had once been. Desks were more cluttered than the last time she had visited, and it looked like the floor hadn't been mopped in a day or two, which was incredibly unlike them.

"Can you tell me what happened?" Ebuka asked Chief Girano privately in his office. She hoped that the discretion would be able to give her a more personal connection to him, providing her with more information than if she were to just ask the entire squad.

"What would you like to know?" he asked, failing to hide the pain in his voice.

"Anything that you'd be willing to share," she replied gently. "Is there anything that you feel would be important for me to know? Or that you feel has been overlooked during the investigative process so far?"

"Before I do that, I'd like to ask you a question," he said, his eyes narrowing.

"What's that?"

"Why do you care? Why are you investigating? This isn't your line of work. It shouldn't matter to you, yet it does. Why?"

Ebuka frowned. "I care about the wellbeing of my people. All of their lives matter, the guards included. As to why I am investigating even though I am a congresswoman, it is because I feel that it is easiest to write legislation that is founded on intelligence that carries a level of credibility.."

Chief Girano smiled. "I like that answer. It's more straightforward than anything I've heard from Congress in a long time."

"We do have a problem with convolution, don't we."

"Yes, you do. Now, to answer your questions. This whole Ragnarok business is not a new thing. Not even a little bit. The guards have been dealing with small cases related to this one word for a while now, and up until this, we just thought that it was a group of kids, possibly a gang. Now, however, it's obvious that this is much, much bigger."

"What kinds of cases was it related to?"

"You want to know if perhaps we can discover a motive for this person slash group?" Chief Girano asked.

Ebuka nodded.

"Well, to put it simply, they don't have a lot in common. Sometimes we will find lost wallets with Ragnarok written on them, and other times it will flash across someone's computer screen. We haven't found a lot of connection between cases, but I have to admit that that is at least in part because we used to think that it didn't matter all that much."

"Do you mind if I help you search for a correlation?" Ebuka asked. "I am quite good at things like that."

Chief Girano squinted and tilted his head. "I don't really know. You haven't been trained in procedure or anything like that. It might not be a good idea."

This frustrated Ebuka, although she wouldn't show it. "Are these cases at least available for public viewing?" she asked.

"Some of them are," Chief Girano replied. "Others are still being kept under wraps because they are open."

"Would you mind pointing me in the direction of the ones that are publicly available?"

Chief Girano smiled. "I like the way you think. I would like to reinforce that you will not be working with the police, although if you can give us some potentially useful information, you will not see me complaining."

"Of course, Chief. I am a public servant, and that means helping any way that I can."

"Some don't see your position the same way that you do."

"Those people shouldn't have power," Ebuka replied frankly. "To use influence to do anything but help is to manipulate."

"Words to live by," Chief Girano nodded.

"Indeed."

"I will have the files sent to your office. I hope you will be able to find something that we were too blind to be able to see."

"I hope so, too. Thank you for your help, Chief. You are a good man."

"And you a good woman."

-5-

After having spent three full days, or rather 72 hours, at her mother's place, Juliette knew that it was time to return home. She hated to admit it, but she was scared to do so. Why, she didn't know. Jacques hadn't done anything to physically harm or threaten her. Yet she felt fear all the same.

A primal part of her was screaming at her to stay away from him, that he would only bring her more pain and frustration. She wanted desperately to listen, but she had been assigned to him for procreation and marriage, and being afraid of a spouse was not a good enough excuse to file for divorce. Unless he did something to cause her serious harm, they wouldn't even consider it, and even then, it wasn't guaranteed.

Aunt Joan and Uncle Pierre had been very open about the fact that they would let her stay with them as long as she wanted, and her mother made a practically identical offer. It was clear to Juliette that they didn't want her to feel trapped in her marriage with Jacques. It was unfortunate that there wasn't anything that any of her family could truly do to curb her anxiety surrounding him.

So, as she did with everything in her life, she sat down and talked to them about it. It wasn't an easy discussion to have, especially since Juliette hated to admit that she needed help, but in the end, she felt that they had given her a lot of good advice that would only make things better in the long run.

Eventually, they had decided that it would be best for her to unwind with a walk through the rainforest conservancy before returning to the house that she shared with Jacques. Once, she had tried to refer to it as home. Presently, she was disillusioned with the fact that she would never feel fully comfortable there.

Uncle Pierre had wanted to join her, but she had refused. It wasn't that she didn't like him; she just knew that she needed to be able to fend for herself. If she couldn't even go out in public without someone there to watch her, how was she supposed to operate at home when no one else was there?

She shuddered at the idea of spending more time with him. Jacques. A devil creature, he seemed to be. Something was wrong with him that she couldn't explain or understand.

Luckily, the second she stepped into the conservancy, all of her fears and frustrations faded to be replaced by amazement. It was magical, being in nature. Not for the first time that week, Juliette found herself jealous of the natives of Old Earth for being able to go into nature whenever they wanted.

The area smelled dirty, but in the best way possible. Birds chirped, water flowed, and it was generally full of the buzz of life. Juliette loved it more than almost anything else in the world. She started down an unfamiliar path with the hope that she might be able to find something that she hadn't seen before. The idea was that every time she went to the rainforest would be new and exciting so that she never grew bored of visiting.

She jumped over a fallen log and stepped into a shallow puddle. Immediately, the water soaked through the outside of her shoes and licked her socks, creeping its way around her feet. It was uncomfortable, but not enough that she would pay it any mind. Everything else was far more important.

Something caught her eye. She stopped in her tracks. An orange ribbon was dangling from a tree. A snake. The specific kind, she couldn't tell, but based on the head shape, Juliette could tell that it wasn't venomous. That was good news. For a second she had been scared of being bitten to death; now she only had to worry about constriction. Nature was amazing.

Careful not to make too much noise, she made her way past it. It appeared that the snake either didn't care about her or was sleeping because it didn't so much as move the entire time it had been in sight.

Further along the path, Juliette caught sight of a small mammal that she couldn't identify. It scurried away from her the minute she had spotted it, but she was fairly certain that it was a species that she had never seen before. Almost nothing about it was familiar, except for perhaps parts of the tail. Maybe she just hadn't gotten a good look at it, though.

She walked even further still, enjoying herself immensely. It felt amazing to be out of the gray boxes that people called houses. They were efficient with their space usage, sure, but besides that, they were abominations. Juliette was beginning to realize more and more that she hated them and only found them bearable because one of them was owned by her family.

Out of nowhere, she tripped on a lump of something and fell to the ground. Blinking, attempting to get her bearings, Juliette looked towards her feet to see what had caused her to fall. There was nothing near her feet, although her legs were covered in a sort of black powder from the knees down. *What is that?* she thought.

She got back to her feet and tried to brush the dust off of her legs with her hands. After a few moments of brushing, she was satisfied and moved to continue walking, stopping herself when she saw that her hands were now covered with the black powder as well.

"What is this shit?" she thought aloud.

Frustrated, she went to a nearby creek to wash herself off. Her best guess was that whatever it was was statically charged and therefore stuck to her with forces beyond that of friction. It was the only thing that made sense unless it was some new sort of sticky black powder that she wasn't aware of.

She stepped into the chilling water, which was barely deep enough to reach her mid-calf, and watched the scenery as she waited for the stream to take the powder off of her. A few bugs fluttered through the air. Some were butterflies, others were simple beetles, but they were mesmerizing all the same.

One look down and all of the happiness she was feeling was diluted by annoyance. The black powder was persistently sticking to her clothes like it had been glued or painted on. Juliette furrowed her brow. What the hell was going on?

If the water couldn't get it off, then there was no use worrying about it. She stepped out of the creek, sloshing through wet steps, and continued onwards down the same path as before. This time, due to how soaked her shoes had become, it was harder not to focus on it and thinking about not thinking about it only drew her attention to the squish of the water even more.

She hated the feeling, but it wouldn't distract her from being able to enjoy the forest. She took a deep breath, waiting for the familiar scents of nature to fill her nostrils. But wait. What was that? *Fire?* she thought.

A haze suddenly filled her vision. The scent of smoke had replaced the natural odors of the rainforest. Juliette felt herself panicking. She couldn't see it, but there was a fire. Hyperventilating, she started to look around, searching for the exit. At this point, the air was too thick for her to see properly, and her eyes began to water.

"No," she whispered. "No. No. No no no no no no no..." She stumbled around as the world swam. "Where's the exit?" she said aloud, feeling her consciousness fade. The last thing she perceived before blacking out was a faint orange glow and the sound of feet against the underbrush.

Juliette awoke, dazed and disoriented. Her head hurt and

she smelled like fire, but otherwise, she felt fine. From what little she could see, it seemed like she was in her room with a silhouette of a person standing next to her.

"Mom?" she asked.

The figure said nothing and turned and left.

Juliette rubbed her head and tried to blink some of the grogginess out of her eyes. She hoped they would adjust soon. She hated not being able to see. Pushing herself up from her bed, some of the pain that she had been unable to notice earlier shot into the forefront of her mind. Her stomach screamed in agony, forcing her to sit back in her bed. The sheets hugged her uncomfortably, reinforcing the idea that she was unable to move much.

"Who is there?" she cried out, sending a shockwave of pain down her chest as she did. "Can you help me?"

Silence. She strained her ears with the hope that they were just busy doing something and would eventually reply. Something deep down told her that she was now alone and there would be no response, but she didn't want to listen to that rational part of her mind. The sound of the front door closing asserted that this was the case, though, and Juliette forced herself to think with logic and without optimism.

She tried to sit up once more, and this time her stomach didn't hurt quite as much. Curious as to what had happened and why she hadn't checked the first time she had felt something, Juliette lifted her shirt to examine the damage. Sure enough, cracks and blisters were running all along her abdomen. It didn't hurt so bad before she had seen it, but now, having witnessed just how disgusting the injury was, Juliette felt a wave of pain wash over her. It was grotesque, and she was miserable in all ways after having seen it.

However, she was strong-willed and self-sufficient enough to force herself to get up and treat herself. Her mouth was dry, her stomach was empty, and presumably that stranger would not be back for her anytime soon.

The pain was there, but she wouldn't let it control her. She took a step and nearly fell to the ground. She hadn't realized how weak she had become. It was frustrating. Steadying herself on the side of her bed, Juliette took another step, this time concentrating on success and using that to fuel her expedition to the kitchen. Her world was torment, but at least she was alive.

-6-

Ebuka was sifting through the pile of information that Chief Girano had given her when Tim burst into the room.

"There's been a fire," he panted. "It was in the rainforest conservancy."

Ebuka was hardly even surprised. It hadn't even been four whole days since the last attack in the French Sector, and there was already another.

She simply looked at him and nodded, then grabbed her coat from where it hung on her chair. The two of them had been cut from the same cloth. They both liked to act, and right then, the only thing that either of them could think to do was to visit the scene of the crime to see if it was related to the Ragnarok case. Briefly, she recognized that she would have been an amazing police officer if her life would have taken her in another direction, but she was happy where she had ended up.

The forest had been completely burnt to a crisp. The creeks had been blocked by ash and debris, filling up the upper levels of the conservancy with water that would eventually trickle out to the other parts of the forest.

In the strangest of ways, Ebuka was beyond ecstatic at the sight of this. Not that there had been a fire, of course, or that such a beautiful piece of the natural world had been destroyed, but rather because the ship was still intact even after a catastrophe of that scale. Throughout her whole lifetime, there had only ever been an accidental fire or two in the conservatories, and none of them had been of the scale of the one that had just happened. It was good that their fire prevention systems were as high-quality as they were.

The guards were already there, of course, accompanied by the maintenance workers that specialized in disasters. From what Ebuka could understand, there was a sort of rivalry between the groups even though they were supposed to work together. Presently, only one guard and one maintenance worker were cooperating while the rest of them shunned each other. So Ebuka migrated toward the two cooperating men.

"This happened because of a maintenance mistake," the guard was saying. "If you would have been watching oxygen levels more closely, you would have been able to stop it from spreading."

"There was clearly an accelerant used, and that's the guard's job to prevent from entering the conservatory," the maintenance worker retorted.

Or perhaps they were only talking because they were fighting. Ebuka laughed. Some things never seemed to change, no matter the situation. "Could it perhaps be both?" she asked, interrupting their counterproductive conversation.

They looked at her simultaneously. "Who are you?" they asked in synchrony.

"Congresswoman Abdullahi," she replied. "And this is my associate, Timothy Drummond. We are here about the fire."

"Would you like me to brief you?" the guardsman jumped in, eager to steal the glory from the maintenance worker.

"No, he'd just botch it," the maintenance worker replied. "I would provide you with objectivity and realistic reasoning behind all of my claims."

"The congresswoman does not have time for bickering," Tim said slowly. "She works efficiently, so if she cannot get this information from one of you, she will not request it from either."

Ebuka stifled a grin. Tim was such a pleasure to be around. He could seemingly read her mind, and it was beautiful. Whenever a tough thing had to be done or said, she knew that she could always rely on him.

The men's faces froze and they turned to each other. It was likely that they had just understood how insignificant their little squabble might have seemed. They still hated each other, but in the presence of one of their congresspeople, it seemed that their patience had extended beyond its normal maximum capacity.

"I can explain the science behind everything that happened, and he can talk to you about the legal stuff," the maintenance worker said finally. "Does that work for the congresswoman?"

Ebuka nodded, her stoic mask covering how entertaining that had been for her.

"Essentially, the rainforest is an extraordinarily humid environment. Because of this, it makes it difficult for fires to start, and unlike temperate rainforests, this tropical one is not quite as flammable. All of this is to say that without a proper accelerant, like petroleum or gunpowder, it would be difficult for a fire of this scale to occur."

Ebuka, of course, knew most of what the worker had just explained to her, but it had been good to get a confirming opinion on it. "And if an accelerant is involved, that implies arson?" Ebuka asked.

The maintenance worker nodded. "It is highly improbable that there would be enough of an accelerant lying around. In fact, I am confident enough in its improbability to say that it is impossible."

"So you're certain that this was arson," Ebuka responded.

"This conversation is approaching the edge of my qualifications, but perhaps he can tell you," the maintenance worker said, nodding towards the guardsman.

"Based on the patterns of the flame, it is difficult to say exactly where the flame started and what the accelerant was, but we can say for near-certainty that this was, in fact, an unlawful burning of a conservancy."

"What kind of motive would push someone to do something like this?" Ebuka asked. "Aren't the conservancies generally well-liked by the public?"

"Generally, yes. Although this could have been an attack against a multitude of things. It seems likely that this is related to the Ragnarok massacre that transpired a few days ago, seeing as it is in the French Sector and of an unheard-of magnitude."

Suddenly, they were approached by a police scientist in a hazmat suit. Ebuka had noticed them when she had first entered the area. They, along with a few other people in similar garb, had been searching through the wreckage, and for what, she didn't know.

"Excuse me, Congresswoman. I have news if you would like to hear."

"Of course. Proceed."

"This is not just an arson, but also another massacre. We just found three corpses within the trees, although it is likely that there are more due to the intensity of the flames and the damage done to the bodies that we found."

"Thank you for informing me. And please, tell the chief that I am grateful for his philanthropic attitude. His donations towards my investigations have been incredibly useful."

"I will let him know," the scientist said with a short nod and then quickly returned to what they had been doing moments before.

Ebuka turned to Tim, her only company now that everyone else had left to continue their work on the crime scene. "This is all tied together, isn't it?"

"Almost certainly. Things are changing, perhaps faster than we can react."

"Perhaps."

Ebuka flipped another folder closed and made a note of the important parts of the case. Like most of the other cases that she had already looked through, there were helpful things, but it felt like there was an important piece missing. There was something behind it all that she knew she wouldn't be able to see without diving deeper into Ragnarok. She just wasn't sure if she was ready for that yet.

So far, all she knew was that there was a group of people related to sabotage going around the station and the word 'Ragnarok.' Other than that, there wasn't much to go on. Why they were sabotaging was still a mystery, and their end goal had yet to be determined.

She felt like she was treading water, analyzing the ripples of an ocean while a hurricane brewed behind the horizon. An overwhelming sense of dread immediately filled her. She was wrong about her analogy, of course. The hurricane had already struck and the dead were beginning to pile up. The eye wall approached, one of the most catastrophic things that humans had ever experienced since before the sun had gone out. Ebuka wasn't sure how she knew that that was the case, but it was. And it was up to her to figure out what was going on so humanity could live to see another 24-hour period of darkness. It was all up to her.

-7-

Juliette opened the beeping control panel, too tired and in pain to care about the error. It said something about how a reactor was operating at 80% percent capacity, but she didn't know what that meant, so she wrote a report and moved on.

She winced as she closed and locked the control panel. She had missed all five of her allotted free days from work already, and she wasn't willing to take time off simply because she had a few small burns. She needed the money, and the station needed her labor.

It had only been a few days since the stranger had visited her in her bed, and she still couldn't get them out of her head. Currently, more than anything, she wanted to know who it had been. It infuriated her that her memory was so fuzzy surrounding the event and that she had been so out of it when they had been there.

Her stomach grumbled. When was the last time she had eaten? She couldn't remember. Certain things just weren't much of a priority anymore, and she wasn't sure why they had fallen into the background of her mind. Eating, sleeping, drinking, and socializing should have been far more important to her, but presently, they meant as little to her as political participation.

It occurred to her right then that she hadn't seen her family in some time, at least not since the accident. *Maybe I should visit them*, she thought. She knew that Mother would be happy to see her, and maybe Father would be back home from work. She hadn't seen him in forever and suddenly missed him more than anything.

Her heart hurting her more than she could bear, Juliette made her way back towards her parent's home in the French Sector. She passed a few people that she thought she recognized, one man in a dark hood that almost seemed familiar, and a few guards. Ever since her accident and the incident with Jacques she had been hypervigilant to the point of insanity. She simply valued her safety too much.

Soon, she was standing on her parents' doorstep, readying to knock. Her hand moved towards the door, but she stopped herself. Something felt wrong. Every instinct in her body was screaming at her to run away from that place, that she would only find pain and horrors beyond her comprehension if she were to enter. Where had that voice come from? The first time she had listened to it had been after the first incident with Jacques and that had been because of how unsafe he had made her feel in her own home. What had happened in her parents' home to make her feel that way?

Shaking with fear and fatigue, Juliette forced herself to go inside. There was an awful, pervasive silence inside. It seemed like it was trying to tear her fear out of her chest in the form of a scream. Her favorite place, her sanctuary from the darkness, was shrouded in shadow.

She opened her mouth to call out to her mother, but her hand rose out of the void to cover it. That wasn't a good idea. The silence was evil, but it would be even worse to interrupt it. Her only option was to fit into it like a piece of a rotting puzzle, hoping that she wouldn't fall out by chance.

The sound of footsteps pierced the silence like a gunshot. Juliette hadn't known it until then, but she had memorized and internalized the sounds of her family's footsteps, and those were foreign. She had never heard them before. There was an intruder.

The Dominion of Life

Juliette turned and looked at the door behind her. She could leave. She could run and save herself, but her family was still inside. She couldn't do that. What if somebody got hurt because she wasn't there to help? She wouldn't be able to live with herself.

Was she even certain that they were home, though? Perhaps she was only sticking around to find out that they were being robbed, and she would be the one to get hurt. That wouldn't be good. So she checked to see if their shoes were where they were usually kept, and sure enough, there they were. According to what little information she had, they were, in fact, home.

A shadow of a person stepped out of Juliette's old room and stood in the hallway for a moment, only to move on to the bathroom. Juliette stood still, keeping her hand over her mouth so that her breathing couldn't make too much noise.

The second the intruder was gone, she dove behind the kitchen counter. The front room was an odd conglomerate of a living room, the kitchen, and the dining room with a hallway through the middle of the back wall that led to the bed and bathrooms. Basically, there weren't a lot of places to hide. She would have noticed if they had been in the front room, so that meant that they had to be in one of the back ones.

She lowered herself to the ground and started to crawl on her elbows and stomach towards the back. She needed more information. As she approached, she could hear the intruder ruffling through the bathroom cabinet. Bottles of various things collided with each other, making hollow metallic noises. The shower curtain was pulled back. The toilet was opened and then closed. Whatever the reason, the intruder was searching for something.

A moment later, the intruder was back in the hallway. Their face was shrouded in shadow, but based on his body shape, Juliette could confidently say that they were a male. In his hand, he held a dagger. It didn't look like any of the knives in their kitch-en from what little Juliette had seen, so it was safe to assume that he had brought it with him. Why would someone invade some-one else's home with a weapon? The answer slammed into her mind almost immediately, bringing with it panic and hatred. To kill someone. Of course, that was why. But who would want to kill her parents? They were such nice people, always doing their best to help others. What had they done wrong? What had they done to deserve something like that? Almost as if he were made of shadow, the man dematerialized, appearing to have stepped into her parents' room.

Terrified that she might lose him, Juliette sacrificed some of her stealth for mobility and rose to her hands and knees. She moved slowly but deliberately, stopping anytime she heard a noise. She tried to quiet her breathing as much as she could, although the more she held her breath, the more she deprived herself of oxygen, and it only resulted in her slightly hyperven-tilating.

Something thudded loudly inside, and Juliette's panic only increased. She heard muffled screams from inside the room and jumped to her feet. No, she shouted in her head. No, they couldn't be hurt. They had to be okay.

She peeked around the corner to see what had happened. She could see her mother tied up with the man holding a knife to her face. He was saying something that she couldn't under-stand, but it sounded threatening. But where was her father? Had he been related to the thud from before?

Juliette thought about jumping into the room to stop him. What if she could take the knife and use it against him? Maybe she could save both of them if she could do that. She knew she couldn't, though. The man was far larger than she was, and she had never been trained to fight. That would just result in her getting hurt, or dying.

The Dominion of Life

The intruder suddenly stopped what he was doing and turned around. Juliette whipped her head away from the threshold, hopeful that she had not been seen. Her heart raced as thoughts of what might happen filled her mind. Was she going to be killed because she saw too much?

But the room was silent. There were no footsteps, no screams, no sounds at all. She wished that she could see into the room without being caught; her curiosity was overwhelming.

Suddenly, the dark figure stuck his head out of the doorway. Juliette shrunk against the wall. *Please, don't see me. Please, don't see me. Please, don't see me*, she repeated to herself. As if someone had listened to her thoughts, the intruder retreated into her parents' room, and she was left alone with heavy breaths and tormentous thoughts once more.

She came to realize then that if she were to be spotted by the intruder, she would not just be hurt, she would be killed. And that was unacceptable. Her parents needed her, and not just because they had an intruder in their home. They needed her love and her care. Nobody would not take her from her family.

A thud sounded from inside her parents' room once more, and the rising tide of confidence inside of Juliette receded. What could she do? Footsteps approached, and her heartbeat quickened once again. Her time for action shortened as each step got closer. What could she do? He was practically at the doorway already. What could she do?

Frantically, and without care for her noise levels, Juliette dove into the bathroom. The sound was deafening to her ears that had adjusted to the quietude, so she sat and waited for the intruder to peek in and end her life.

The footsteps were in the hallway now, and from where she sat in the bathroom, Juliette could just barely make out the shape of the man. Was he staring at her or looking the other way? Had her attempt at remaining unseen only revealed her to him?

The intruder stood there for a moment, unmoving, and then reached into his back pocket and pulled out a small tablet. Its light shone brightly, illuminating his face with a faint blue glow. He appeared to be European and had a large scar running down the side of his face. His nose was flattened and his eyes looked tired.

And then, as if nothing had happened, he tucked his phone in his pocket, turned away, and left the home. Juliette felt a pang of hatred as the door gave a familiar click upon his departure. The nonchalance behind his actions was horrifyingly awful, and she wished that she had the power to… do something to him. Anything.

Now that he was gone, Juliette jumped up, flipped on the lights, and sprinted to her parents' room. They had to be okay. There had been an intruder and that had been scary, but everything was going to be okay. Soon they would all be talking like they usually did.

Her hope died in her heart the second she flipped the lights on in their room. Bloodstains. Dismembered limbs. She heard a sob come from somewhere. Her mind could hardly even process any of what she was looking at. The sight was so horrifying that the lights seemed to listen to her and shut off. Unable to understand what had happened or why, Juliette fell to the ground and hugged her knees, praying that soon her arms would be joined by theirs. It had to all have been in her imagination. It had to have all been a dream. They weren't dead. They were always there for her. They couldn't be dead.

-8-

Ebuka was beginning to grow tired of just how much was going wrong aboard *the Dominion of Life*. High-profile criminal cases had skyrocketed over the past week. Presumably, something was connecting it all, but Ebuka couldn't see it yet. She could see the fear on the faces of each person she passed in the halls. It hurt her soul to see. Her job was to protect them and make their lives better, and there was nothing she could do to make them happier other than continuing her work.

And it only hurt that much more when the crime was committed against someone that she knew personally. Finding Juliette Lavigne in the fetal position next to the remains of her parents was perhaps one of the saddest things that Ebuka had ever seen.

She had tried to comfort the girl, but she knew that such an event was inconsolable. There was nothing that Ebuka could say or do to make Juliette feel any better. The most important people in her life had just been ripped from her grasp, and violently at that.

The girl had been unresponsive when the guards had tried to talk to her, so Ebuka had offered to let her stay with them until she was less vacant. They had talked about taking her home, but at the sound of this, Juliette had objected vocally, likely her only words since her parents had passed away.

So there Juliette sat, wrapped in a blanket in Ebuka's office. She was in Tim's chair, leaving the man to sit on the floor. It had been hours since they had arrived, and during that time Ebuka hadn't let the girl out of her sight. Not that she had made any indication that she wanted to move, though. Shock still had a strong hold on Juliette.

Tim got up from where he sat and stood next to Ebuka at her desk. "She won't be talking for quite some time," he whispered. "I'd wager that she isn't even lucid enough to recognize that I'm saying anything. You should go home and get some sleep. I can watch her."

Ebuka wanted to jump at the offer and get some much-needed rest in her bed. It felt like it had been an eternity since she had been allowed to truly relax, and the prospect of it appealed to her greatly. But she knew she couldn't leave.

"I appreciate that," she said, suddenly aware of just how tired she was. "I want her to see me when she comes to, though. I want her to trust me so she can tell me what she knows."

"That sounds manipulative," Tim replied.

"Manipulating people to help them isn't evil," was all she could think to respond with.

"And I was not passing any judgment upon you. I was merely making an observation."

Ebuka nodded slowly and then set her head down on her desk. It was so comfortable.

"Would you like any coffee?" Tim asked. "It could help."

"No, I'm fine," Ebuka replied, barely aware of the fact that she was drifting off. She had more to say, to ask, but her mouth didn't seem to want to move anymore. It was far too comfortable where it was. She hoped that Tim would be able to understand what she wanted, although she had already forgotten what that was. She felt Tim tap her on the head. His touch was warm and tingly, and she wished that he wouldn't have stopped. How lonely was she, who had everything?

Ebuka tore open a present and grinned. A calculator. She

squealed in delight and ran over to hug her mother. That had been the only thing she had wanted. Everything else would make her happy, too, of course, although not quite like the calculator.

It was her eighth birthday party. She had been talking about the calculator all year, practically. Ever since her older sister had received her own computer, Ebuka couldn't stop thinking about the idea of data analysis. It sounded so fun, to be able to know what people liked just based on a few numbers. The way it had been described to her had made it seem magical, and the idea of working with it excited her to no end.

Riding the high that came from opening the calculator, young Ebuka greedily tore the wrapping paper off another present. Her family watched with happiness in their eyes. Her father was always so supportive of her, as were her sisters and mother, but he was just different. There was something about him that made her feel safe like she could say or do anything and he would still love her.

Even when the wrapping paper was almost completely off of the present, Ebuka still had no idea what it was. It seemed like it was a book of some kind, but it wasn't one that she had ever seen before. She gently peeled off the last bits of paper and looked at her mother with confusion.

"What is it?" she asked. The title read 'The Falseness of the Final Flicker.' It was by a man named Luc Lightbringer, which seemed like a strange enough name to assume that it was not the man's real one.

"Read the back," her mother said eagerly.

With a forced smile, Ebuka turned the paperback over and did as her mother had requested. 'The world didn't ask to live on. This choice was thrust upon humanity. We were meant to perish with the flames of the sun, frozen by the frost of death. Our time has passed, and now it is our duty to give us the fate that we should have been met with.'

"We should have died on Earth?" she asked, more confused than ever. Her father's expression of happiness fell away immediately, replaced by one of concern.

"What is that?" he asked, reaching to take it out of her hands before Ebuka could reply. "Oh, it's a fantasy book," he said with a slight smile after flipping through it for a second. "I was worried."

Ebuka's mother frowned. "No-"

"Yeah, I can't believe I thought it was anything else," her father interrupted. "This Luc Lightbringer guy seems to be tackling some interesting issues."

Ebuka's mother seemed frustrated by this and appeared to want to argue with Father, but she never did. It seemed like they had some unspoken agreement that the situation would be left alone for the time being. Ebuka wished she understood what was happening. She got the feeling that what was going on was significant to all of their lives, but she didn't know enough to know how or why. Her ignorance agitated her to no end, and she would work very hard to make sure that she never felt that way again.

The rest of her party went on without any other problems. In fact, Ebuka was growing suspicious of how little conflict there was. There should have been a little arguing here and there, but there wasn't. None of the social interactions felt natural and she found that she was no longer enjoying her party. Later she would recognize how strange her relationship with discord was, however as a child, she had no understanding of this.

The night dragged on, and finally, the party ended. Ebuka scurried to her room with all of her gifts, excited to lay them out and play with them. Most of all, she couldn't wait to use the calculator. She had already read the manual front to back three times and was confident that she had a pretty solid grasp of how to work it. The other gifts were cool, too. They just didn't compare to the calculator.

When she finally had all of her gifts in a pile on her bed, sorting them by type, then by size, then by color, she realized that her father had never given her that book back. She thought about going and asking him for it; after all, she had gotten it as a present, not him. Eventually, she became far too enthralled with her gifts to leave and ask him for it, and it faded into the depths of her mind where it would be forgotten. Just another book that she hadn't read.

Ebuka's head shot off of her desk. The world was incoherent and her mind even more so. How had she forgotten about that book? She hadn't seen it since her eighth birthday, but the more she thought about it, the more it felt important.

Her vision cleared moment by moment, allowing for some clarity. Juliette was there with her, still, which was good. Tim sat on the floor and was reading through the cases that Ebuka hadn't managed to get to. She was grateful that he was so diligent even when she wasn't there to direct him.

"Could you stay with her while I go run an errand?" she asked him as she pushed herself out of her chair.

"Of course," he replied. "Before you go, though, can you come look at something that I think I've discovered?"

Ebuka walked over to where he sat and looked over his shoulder at the papers on the ground. It was strange to her that they still used paper files when digital ones were available, but it seemed that that was one of the archaic parts of Old Earth that they hadn't forgotten.

"I took all of the cases that I could find and ordered them chronologically. Then, I tried to take specific things about them that were consistent and see if there were any patterns. The first things I looked at were dates, then locations and crimes. Finally

I started to dig into random details at each crime scene."

"Did you find anything?"

"Yeah. At each scene, they would leave a small letter, it seems. At first, I dismissed this as an abnormality, maybe even a calling card. But I linked them all together to create this message."

He picked a note off of the ground and handed it to her. It read "Vji xusmf xomm ipf op etj epf gmeni cz vji xomm ug Tasvas. Xjip Jiewip gemmt, finupt xomm tviq uav ug vjios hsewit vu tvsephni zua xovj vjios optepovz. Ov xomm ci hmusouat."

Ebuka frowned. "And this looks like something to you?" she asked skeptically.

He nodded furiously. "This is one of the most basic cryptograms that I've ever had the pleasure of learning. For whatever reason, our culprit is attempting to maintain some level of secrecy but doesn't care too much if they are found."

"What does it say?"

"The world will end in ash and flame by the will of Surtur. When Heaven falls, demons will step out of their graves to strangle you with their insanity. It will be glorious." he explained. "Not exactly subtle. I have a slight feeling I know what Ragnarok is."

Ebuka was absolutely astounded. She would need to check his work, but coincidences like that didn't just happen. If he had found such a coherent message directly related to the events of Ragnarok as stated in mythology, there was an impossibly low chance that he was wrong.

"How did you even think to do something like this?" she asked.

Tim tilted his head. "Well, usually with fanatical groups like this, they do things for attention. They like to leave clues and pull people into their movements so that they garner a sort of maniacal popularity. I did what superfans of TV shows and books did back on Old Earth and started to theorize."

"That's brilliant," Ebuka said. "Absolutely brilliant."

"Thank you."

"I need to go now, but can you call Chief Girano and let him know what you found? Maybe we can decode more of the information that they've given us."

"I will."

Ebuka stepped out of the room, unable to fully comprehend the genius that she had just witnessed. How had she not seen that side of her associate until then? She had always just assumed that he was around her intelligence, maybe slightly dumber, but that one act was something she felt that she never could have even thought of.

-9-

Juliette felt some of the pressure on her chest go away at the exact moment that Congresswoman Abdullahi left the room. It was almost magical. Something about Tim's presence was completely calming, reminding her of the way that her mother had consoled her when she had still been alive. At the thought of her parents, she expected to be filled with grief once more, however, that was not the case. She was sad, yes, although it wasn't uncontrollable.

"What is going on?" she asked. There were strange holes in her memory that she couldn't explain. Her stomach grumbled, reminding her that she was hungry, and her head ached for some unknown reason.

Tim got up and reached into Ebuka's desk, pulling out a container. He took the cap off and retrieved a single pill, which he offered casually to Juliette.

"For your head," he elaborated before she had the chance to ask another question.

She held it in her hand awkwardly as he went and got her a cup of water. When he returned, she downed the water with the medicine in one gulp and wiped the excess from around her mouth with her sleeve.

"Thank you," she responded.

"Would you like to have a conversation?" Tim asked her after sitting down on the ground and starting to look over a bunch of scattered papers.

"What would we talk about?"

"Any topic under the stars. Whatever you would like, really."

Juliette thought. She wanted to ask why she couldn't remember anything since seeing her parents dead, hopeful that he may be able to provide her with some answers.

"Might I offer a suggestion, though?" he asked, interrupting her thoughts.

She nodded.

"Perhaps you would like to talk about what happened after leaving your parents' abode? I know with a lot of people, shock can do some crazy things, blurring certain events in the mind."

Juliette blinked with astonishment. That had been the second time in a few minutes that he had practically read her mind. Maybe he was just good at his job as an assistant and was simply trying to serve her the way he served Congresswoman Abdullahi. Yes. That made sense to her.

"So what happened then?"

"You know your parents were killed, yes?"

She nodded, waiting for tears to form in her eyes. They never did.

"You know that there was an intruder?"

She nodded again.

"It's just after this that you don't know about, then?"

"Yes."

Tim took a deep breath. "I am going to fill you in, although I'm not sure it will even be that important to you."

"Why not?"

"In fact, I am certain that you will hardly care at all."

Juliette felt herself growing frustrated. The calm that had once been in control of her was fading, it seemed. "Can you just tell me?" she asked, unable to mask the impatience in her tone.

Tim smiled. "You just proved my point, I guess."

"What?"

"You long for what you do not have. And to know that you once had something and no longer have it does not just bother you, it infuriates you. Case in point, you are angry that I am withholding this information from you that you should know but you don't."

Juliette furrowed her brow. "So now I'm the subject of an experiment?"

"Not an experiment," he disagreed. "More like a demonstration."

They sat in silence for a moment. Juliette couldn't tell if she liked him or not. There was something comforting about his presence, but at the same time, every time he spoke, it rubbed her the wrong way.

"If I annoyed you, I apologize," he said. "I tend to find certain things fascinating, and what we talked about was one of them."

"I understand," she replied, even though she wasn't sure that she did. "Where did Congresswoman Abdullahi go?"

"Hm? Oh. You mean Ebuka? She went to run an errand and should be back soon. Why?"

"I wonder if perhaps she and I would have a more productive conversation," Juliette said, trying her best to not be rude.

"Maybe so," Tim admitted. "I have been accused by many of being rather irritating and difficult to talk to."

"They're wrong," she responded. "You're not difficult to talk to; you're difficult to learn from."

"I think I rather like that distinction," Tim said absentmindedly. "However, it could be argued that those two are not as different as you say. Isn't conversation just an exchange of information, meaning that everyone is teaching and learning whenever they talk to anyone?"

Juliette didn't reply. There was no use. He seemed like the kind of person to be interested in the most mundane things.

"Do you have any more questions?" he asked.

Juliette searched through her head and found that she did.

Quite a few at that. She hoped that Tim would be able to answer them.

"Why would anyone want to kill my parents"

Tim opened his mouth to speak, but he said no words. He seemed to be thinking about how to answer her question. The sting of disappointment struck Juliette like a viper and she set her head down, waiting for a noncommittal answer.

"I can tell you the answer to that if you would like," he said softly. "If I tell you that, though, you have to promise me that you don't tell anyone how you know these things. I'm not supposed to know them myself."

At that moment, Juliette got the feeling that Tim was more than he seemed. How did he know so much? It was a question that she knew would plague her for the rest of her life and she doubted that she would ever know the truth.

"I want to know the truth," Juliette replied with more conviction than anything she had ever uttered before. "I *need* to."

Tim nodded slowly, looking at his hands and then up at her. Within his eyes, she saw something. It might have been fear, or maybe even regret, but behind it all, she could see that he was not well and that something was eating at his soul. It was terrifying and beautiful all at the same time.

"Your father was not who you thought him to be," Tim began. "From what I read in his file, he was listed as mining personnel, although I need you to know that for the majority of his life, this was not the case. Andre Fontaine was, in reality, a revolutionary. There were times when he mined, but these times were short and he does not remember much from them. Luckily for his hatred for this profession, he had quite a few connections that would lead him to join an iconoclastic group. The same group, might I add, that Ebuka and I are hunting down right now."

Juliette wanted to ask questions, to object to what she was

hearing. Her father couldn't have been lying to her. He was a good man. He had always been there for her and their family, providing them with laughter and joy when they needed it most. She didn't want to interrupt him, though, so she remained quiet.

"He, unlike others, did not join this group to fulfill its purpose. Instead, he sought companionship and the benefits that it gave him. As a result of his membership, he overcame quite a few challenges that your family likely would have been unable to make it through otherwise.

"Unfortunately, the organization eventually found out about his disingenuity. They wanted him to pay for his exploitation and approached him under the guise of trying to find a peaceful solution. They berated him with veiled threats, which your father was incapable of recognizing. You found your parents when these threats were being fulfilled."

"Why are you being so vague about what he did and what happened?" Juliette asked.

Tim pursed his lips. "Knowledge can be a curse," he said after a pause. "I do not wish to burden you with unseemly details. I also fear that I have already told you too much and do not wish to draw further attention to myself."

"Are you a member of this organization?" Juliette blurted out. The question had been at the back of her mind ever since he had started talking about her father.

"I cannot answer that with honesty. You would not believe me, and it would not lead to productive conversation. Your world is so small and simple."

She scoffed. "So I wouldn't understand, then? Do you call me a fool? A little girl who cannot handle the complexities of the world?"

"Yes. But that isn't just you. Few can."

"You're above everyone else? Are you saying that you're a superior being?"

Tim looked at her with deep sincerity and sadness in his gaze. "And sometimes I wish that I weren't."

-10-

Ebuka was getting angrier than she would have liked to admit. She had been searching through the main database of the station for the better part of the day, and still she couldn't find so much as the simplest record of the book that her father had given her. As far as it was concerned, the tome didn't even exist.

If the dream hadn't felt so lucid and important, she would have given up and gone back to the office already. The subconscious mind couldn't always be trusted, after all. She wasn't the superstitious type and was already questioning why she was suddenly so fixated on this book. There was something about it that tickled her mind as if it were awakening a memory that she had long suppressed or forgotten.

It occurred to her that the easiest way to confirm if the events had been real or imagined would be to talk to someone she remembered being there. Her mother and sister weren't a possibility for a myriad of reasons, so that left some of her childhood friends, who she was no longer in contact with, and her father.

She didn't need to linger on the problem much longer before deciding to go to her father. It was a good idea for a lot of reasons, the principal ones being that she had been procrastinating seeing him for far too long, and he had been the one to take the book from her. The chances of him remembering it would be much higher than, say, her friend Abiona.

Admittedly, she was scared to visit him. She searched for ways that she could get out of going but stopped herself before her mind got too far down that road. She needed to see him. A meeting was overdue. There was no doubt in her mind that he missed her the same way she did him; she just didn't like to see how far he had fallen. It wasn't how she liked to remember him.

The Progenitor of Torment was one of the most terrifying places that Ebuka could imagine. In her mind, it was the absolute epitome of terror and torture. The things that went on there were truly awful, and the only reasons she dwelled on it longer than in passing thought were that it was the home of her father, and she was a member of Congress.

In her opinion, the prison represented everything that was wrong with the world. Where it could have been merciful, it was brutal and ruthless, punishing prisoners for even the most basic transgressions. She had no doubt in her mind that there would be political revolutions in the future regarding their treatment. It would, of course, be preferred for those movements to come sooner, but the public didn't care enough yet. One day, though.

She rode in her pod to the station, which flew at a much lower altitude than *the Dominion of Life*. The idea was that if people were to escape, they would have to fight Jupiter's gravity just to get to the only other human colony in the universe. Apparently, the engineers for it hadn't liked the idea of keeping their criminals and their law-abiding citizens living in the same area, so they had segregated them. In principle, Ebuka liked the idea, but in practice, this separation only led to corruption and exploitation. She dreaded what awful things she might see upon this visit.

The pod docked at *the Progenitor*. Ebuka took a deep breath to calm herself, achieving the opposite result. The air felt thicker, like the rottenness of the people inside had infected the very fabric of the universe. She could not wait to leave. Any time spent there was far too long.

She waited for the airlocks to equalize and then stepped into the hallway where she was met by a pair of guards and the warden, whose name she had yet to learn. She was slightly ashamed of this fact, although they would never know that. From their perception, she would be a paragon of professionality and pragmatism. The idea that she might not be privy to certain information would likely not even occur to them.

In a deep, evil quietude, they led her to the visiting area, which was reserved specifically for high-level government positions, such as hers and the police. It was their policy that they didn't allow normal citizens to interact with such hardened criminals, as they believed this to be a breeding ground for rebellious ideas. Of course, this only forced people to commit crimes so that they could see their family members, but it was likely that the warden either didn't see this, didn't care, or was actively encouraging this behavior. Ebuka thought it was rather telling that she was so evenly split among the three.

The hallway opened up into a wide-open area in which all of the inmates could be seen in their soundproof glass cells. It was as if they were zoo animals and the guards were simply tourists enjoying a day out. The inmates looked miserable, hateful of everyone and everything that they saw. Ebuka supposed that she couldn't blame them. She would feel the same way if she was placed in a sensory deprivation chamber for the rest of her sane life.

A scream echoed through the room. Ebuka whipped around, hoping to see where it had come from, but the guards seemed unfazed and maybe even amused. What was going on? She was embarrassed by how easily her mask of perfection had fallen and did her best to reapply it, hopeful that the guards hadn't noticed her reaction.

She did a quick scan of the inmates in the glass housings,

wondering if she could perhaps see her father. He was among those, she knew; it was just where specifically that she did not. How long had he been there? 20, maybe 30 years? She couldn't remember anymore. Well, that wasn't true. He had been there since 2113, and it was currently 2141. So 28 years, then.

Would he even know her? Would he recognize her? Would he have gone insane? Would he remember the betrayal he had experienced from her sister and mother and his imprisonment as a result? Ebuka wasn't sure what exactly he had been subjected to during his incarceration, just that it was likely more horrific than anything she had ever witnessed besides, perhaps, the massacre of the French Sector. That had been something else entirely.

The observation room, where guards had been watching with entertained smiles, ended and Ebuka stepped into the room of visitation. It was painted in mostly dull blues and grays with metal bars lining the walls. From her understanding of things, this was entirely for aesthetic reasons as they had access to stronger glass and electromagnetic collar detainment systems than those bars. All they did was make the area feel that much more depressing. She hated it.

The warden motioned for her to sit down, and when she did not, he smiled an awful smile and sat anyway. From there it was easy to see just how fat he was. His stomach rolled over his legs almost as if he were wearing a thick, winter coat from Old Earth. If Ebuka didn't have the sensibility not to, she would have teased him for his weight, if only because she hated how the inmates were being treated.

"Who are you here to see today?" he asked in a New England accent, almost as if he didn't already know the answer to that question.

"Just go get him," Ebuka grumbled. She hated dealing with him already and had barely been talking to him for more than

30 seconds.

"I'm afraid I cannot go get him since I do not know who you mean," the maggot said with the biggest shit-eating grin.

Ebuka marched over to where he was seated and grabbed him by the front of his collar. Usually, she didn't resort to violence, but there was something special about the warden. His face was oddly punchable, and she found that at that moment, there was nothing she wanted more than to hurt him. *The Progenitor of Torment* was already infecting her mind. She needed to leave, and soon.

"What?" she hissed. "Do you want me to belittle myself by saying this to you? Do you truly believe that there is something about admitting that my father is in prison that has any impact on how I view myself? You are an embarrassment. If I were your mother I would have killed myself because of how little my efforts to accomplish anything mattered. Fuck you."

Ebuka could feel her hatred seeping out of her with every breath she took. He was a horrible person and deserved everything that she had said, but there was still a part of her that felt bad for her words. Not that she regretted saying any of it, but there was a part of her that empathized with the maggot. It wasn't a good thing in the sense that he didn't deserve it, however, these feelings did prove that she hadn't fully succumbed to the evil of *the Progenitor*, so she was grateful.

"That's it?" the warden asked, raising an eyebrow. "How disappointing. I expected more from you, Ebuka Abdullahi. You march in with hatred in every aspect of your being, and that's all you could muster? I have heard stories of your legendary will to do good and was expecting something of that sort, not of an adolescent attempting to hurl insults across the playground. Perhaps next time you will be more prepared."

Ebuka wanted to hurt him so badly that it hurt. Or rather, her nails were digging into her palms because of how tightly she was squeezing her hands into a fist. "Just go get my father so I can get out of this shithole faster," she said, letting him go.

"I will have one of my people do it," he replied, evening out his shirt as he rose to his feet. "In the meantime, I would love to keep talking to you."

Ebuka scowled but did not bite. He was trying to irritate her. It wouldn't work, though. Not anymore. He had done what she needed him to do, so now she just had to sit and exist until her father arrived. That sounded simple enough.

"I remember the first time your father broke," the warden said as if they both looked back fondly upon those times. "It was magnificent. His heart carried memories from an irrecoverable time, and with his sanity, those too faded. I'm grateful that I was blessed enough to witness something like that."

Her silence felt weak as if she were losing to him in some sort of abstract battle. So instead of trying to think about her hatred for him or the future, Ebuka tried to focus on her breathing. In. Out. The rhythmic action was calming, giving her something to do while she waited.

At last, the maggot stopped talking and stepped away as her father was escorted into the room. He looked like he was okay, however, she worried that perhaps he had shattered beneath the surface. He was large, taller, and thicker than the average man, which was evidently something that the prison had been unable to steal from him.

The guards pushed him into the now-empty seat that the warden had once been sitting in. Up closer, his pain and torment were far more obvious. Ebuka couldn't begin to understand how she felt about seeing him. It was too much.

"How are you?" she asked.

He just stared at the wall vacantly.

She had expected something like that. It was best to pretend like this wasn't her father any longer, but simply a being that could have the information that she desired. Sure, parts of him might still be around, but it wasn't intelligent to focus on the hope that those parts would dominate their interactions.

"Do you know who I am?" Ebuka pondered, more to herself than to him.

"I- I have had a lot of time to think," he said with a startling clarity behind his words. "I have been granted an eternity, gifted it for the purpose of discovering something. I feel that I am on the verge of knowing what my purpose is, I just need to spend more time in solitude to figure it out. They must send me back. I have already spoken to you for too long."

He got up to leave, but the guards forced him back to being seated. Ebuka was grateful for that. Without their help, she imagined that it would have been impossible to get him to talk.

"Do you remember your name, inmate?" Ebuka asked, wondering if he was even able to recognize that she was talking. She despised the fact that she had just referred to her father as 'inmate,' but it had to be done.

"I can't stay!" he shouted, appearing to panic. "My cell cannot remain empty for this long! It requires me to be there for me to be alive!"

Ebuka decided to take a risk and place one of her hands on his. "You will be perfectly fine. We suspended those systems so that you could talk to me. I needed to talk to you because your mind has advanced so much. You are our only hope."

His eyes softened. "I am?"

The innocence behind his words broke Ebuka's heart in two. Why did she have to lie? Why couldn't he have been normal again?

"Yes, you are. Your purpose, which I am sure you have already figured out, is to answer a series of questions."

He nodded vigorously. "Yes, that's it, exactly."

"I have come with the questions. Are you ready to fulfill

your reason for living?"

He nodded once again.

"I should add that this is only one minuscule part of your purpose. The beginning, I suppose. So prepare yourself for all of the greatness that is to come after." His eyes grew wide at this, and Ebuka felt some sort of relief. She had immediately regretted referring to that conversation as his purpose for living as it made it seem like once it was over he could die, and she wasn't ready for that.

"Well obviously," he replied.

She took a deep breath, for dramatic effect more than anything. "That book that you took from your daughter's eighth birthday party, what was it and why did you take it from her?"

Her father's face fell. "How am I supposed to remember?..." He paused. "Wait. Maybe I know what you mean. Are you talking about Ebuka? Or? I need to think. What book could you possibly mean?"

"You know," was all Ebuka said.

Her father looked distraught. "I don't!" he said indignantly, or was it fearfully? Either way, he was extraordinarily unhappy with what he was hearing.

Ebuka sighed. It seemed his mind was too broken for something like that to still be memorable for him. It hurt, but it made sense. The brain could only recall so much information, and after being tortured for so long, that amount diminished and changed.

Should she leave him? Should she give up? Maybe all of that stuff didn't even matter and she was listening to her subconscious for no reason. *But it felt like somebody was trying to tell me something*, she thought.

Conflicted, she looked her father up and down once more. She could see his fatigue and loneliness plastered upon his skin in the layer of sweat that coated him. It hurt her to see him like that. She would have been lying if she said that she didn't regret seeing him if only a little bit. Suddenly, the name the Progenitor of Torment made so much more sense to her.

"The only thing that I can think of is a book called 'The Falseness of the Final Flicker,'" her father said, setting his head down on the table. "My mind is not what it once was. I apologize for my incompetence."

Ebuka perked up at this. That sounded exactly right. Feeling herself growing excited, she forced herself to stay calm until she was at least out of the prison. She still had more questions to ask.

"Where would I be able to find that book?" she asked. "Would you still have back home, or would it be located elsewhere?"

"I keep it safe," he said. "I can't have Ebuka finding it. She can't get involved. She's too young. She's far too young for something like that. I can't have her getting involved."

Ebuka tuned him out as he started to repeat that over and over again. It was a reminder that he still cared in his own, insane, way; however, that wasn't important at the moment. No matter how much she wanted her father to be there, he wasn't anymore, and Ragnarok was still a pressing issue.

Further conversation was no longer productive, it seemed. Upset but unwilling to show it, Ebuka motioned to the guards that they could take her father back to his cell. She wished that she didn't have to be the one to subject him to that torture.

"No!" he shrieked as they escorted him out. "Don't take me! I still have more to give, more to do! My thoughts aren't enough anymore! I need to act!"

Ebuka clenched her fist, focusing on her hand so that she didn't have to think about him. He was long gone, it seemed. The heartbreak seeped through anyways, though, and as she walked away, she forced herself not to look back. There was no return to him.

The hallway greeted her grief soullessly, a reminder of just how horrible the entire station was. She tried to avoid the gazes of the inmates as she walked by them again, their pained looks hurting her heart and their smiles hurting her heart even more. The world was a cruel, cruel place.

She needed to get out.

At last, she arrived at the airlock that she had docked at. A pod was leaving. She watched as it soared through the sky, passing into the void. It was beautiful. How easily it could depart from its problems, from the evil that it was attached to. Ebuka was envious of this ability. She, on the other hand, felt as if she were cursed to be stuck with the horrific things attached to humanity with no real solace. Help would be brought to the people via her hand, but it would never truly stop all of the malice. She was just a preventer. No matter how hard she fought, death and torment would always win.

"I'm ready to go," she called out, looking for the guards.

No one answered.

"Hello?"

Silence spoke to her still.

Confused, Ebuka walked to the control panel. Perhaps she could just open the airlock and send herself back. It didn't seem too hard.

Messing with the buttons for a bit, she eventually got the inner door to the airlock open. Luckily, both sides of the wall had been equalized before the door was opened. She had heard stories of intense depressurization leading to ships being imploded and didn't want to experience that firsthand.

But where the pod should have been, there was an apparent empty space. Ebuka blinked, immediately aware of the fact that she had been betrayed. By whom and for what purpose, she didn't know, just that they had taken her pod, likely with the hopes of leaving her stranded on the Progenitor of Torment.

Suddenly, a deafening alarm blared, making Ebuka jump just a little. **ESCAPE ATTEMPT**, it screamed. **ESCAPE ATTEMPT. LOCKDOWN PROTOCOL ACTIVATED.**

The alarm quieted for a moment, and Ebuka thought that she had been granted relief until she heard his voice. "Ebuka Abdullahi, defeated by a simple warden," the maggot grunted over the intercom. "So sad to see. Perhaps here, you and your father can be broken together. What a concept, being reunited with him. I would very much like to see that. How unfortunate it is that Ragnarok approaches."

-11-

Jacques Lavigne hated himself. Lying there on the floor of the bathroom after what felt like the thousandth time getting his shit rocked by a bunch of idiots, he cried, wondering what he had done wrong. Why did they view him with such disdain? Blood dripped from his face into his mouth, reminding him all the more of his failure.

He could never understand how things like that were allowed on *the Dominion of Life*. Wasn't the station supposed to be the last hope for humanity? A place where people went to be reminded of why life was good and worth living? At thirteen, he was already all too aware of how much of a lie those words had been. Nothing was pure about humanity. It was a curse, destroying everything it came in contact with. It deserved the death that the sun had attempted to grant it.

Everything hurt, but he forced himself to get up anyway. There was no use lying in his own blood and urine if he could avoid it. His pride, or what little was left of it, prevented him from being that pathetic.

Limping, Jacques walked out of the bathroom and into the school which had quickly become his hell. He wanted to cry, to scream, to rage, but that would just give them the satisfaction of knowing that they had won, so his face remained impassive and cold. Forever cold, to hide the monster that he wished to become. Soon, they would know pain. Soon, they would know fear. And Jacques would be the one to impart it upon them.

12 O'CLOCK, a voice informed him. There were still a few hours until school was over. Jacques looked down upon himself. He couldn't go back to class looking like that. How would the others react, knowing him to be a pitiful piece of shit that was just the punching bag of some morons? He wouldn't be able to live with himself.

Filled with conflict and fury, Jacques limped his way to the front of the school. His heart rate quickened as he stepped through the front doors, hopeful that he wouldn't be stopped. He heard his father's voice in his head. *Confidence is the catalyst for change*, the older man hissed.

Jacques listened, as he always did, and made his way home as if that were where he belonged. People would notice that he was skipping, but he didn't care. It only mattered that he got out of there before people started to ask questions.

He stopped at his front door before entering. Inside, he would either find solace and rest or hell. It was truly one or the other, and he had no way of knowing which. Cautiously, he stepped through the door and took his shoes off, careful not to make too much noise in case the monster was home.

Light on the balls of his feet, as his father had taught him, Jacques made his way to his bedroom where he would be able to change and erase some of the evidence of what had happened. No one could find out.

Quickly, he stripped his clothes off and grabbed another outfit from his dresser. About to go to the bathroom where he would be able to clean himself and change, he heard a noise come from outside his room.

He wanted to scream, to end everything before the monster got him. Why was it there now? Wasn't it supposed to be away, in hell, the place that it bragged about so much? It wasn't supposed to be home. But Jacques knew well enough to know that the monster had made sure to never be home consistently to insight fear in them. It was working too well.

He looked at his change of clothes and wondered if he would be able to just put them on and have that be a sufficient disguise, but he knew that he couldn't. His face was bloody, his legs smelled of fecal matter. His options were limited and growing smaller with each passing minute.

"Jacques?" the monster called out. "Why are you home?"

Jacques' arm started to shake uncontrollably, a side effect of the fear that the monster so lovingly liked to pass along as if it were a gift.

He remained silent, afraid that if he were to respond, the monster would find and hurt him. Maybe if he stayed silent, it would forget about him and move on. Perhaps then, he could shower and clean himself. Perhaps after that, he could relax. He wasn't too stupid to know that this was all wishful thinking though and hated how surprised he felt when the monster screamed again.

"JACQUES!" the voice roared as it always did if there was no response after the first call. "COME OUT RIGHT NOW! I KNOW THAT YOU'RE HOME!"

Jacques was shaking so much that he could barely stand now. The weakness from his beating earlier was not doing him any favors. A tiny part of him wanted to run out and scream at it, asking why it was tormenting him, but he was not a fool. So instead, he hid in his closet like any reasonable person would do.

He took a deep breath, allowing the mustiness and mold to envelop him like the hugs that he had heard so much about. It comforted him, if only slightly, as he waited for the dreaded third call from the monster and the calamity that would come after.

His door clicked open, and Jacques squeezed his eyes shut. *Please*, he thought. *Please, just this time, don't find me. Please, leave me alone so I can rest. I'm so tired. Please.*

A tear streaked down his face. He wasn't ready. Not yet. He couldn't have the monster see his weakness or his failure. Not yet. He needed to calm down and clean himself first.

The closet door clicked open, and the horrible face of his father appeared in the crack of light. Jacques almost whimpered but stopped himself. That would only make things worse. He had to remain stoic and strong as he had learned if this was going to go smoothly; which of course, he knew that it wouldn't.

"There you are, you little shit," his father said with a scowl so awful that Jacques nearly peed himself again. "Why don't you come on out so we can talk about this."

Jacques flinched at these words, wincing as his father reached in and pulled him out before he had any time to respond. That was the way things went around there, and Jacques was used to that. Better to be prepared for the worst than surprised when it came to fruition.

"You smell like weakness, maggot," his father snarled as he sniffed Jacques. "What happened to you?"

Jacques knew better than to answer truthfully. Admitting to being beaten up was the worst possible thing he could do then, so he kept his mouth shut. He hoped he was creative enough to come up with a reasonable lie. That strategy had never worked in the past, but it didn't mean that it couldn't work at all.

"Tell me what happened or you're gonna regret your insubordinate attitude," the monster snarled. "This should be easy. Stop making things harder than they have to be."

Jacques' mind exploded with retorts. He wanted to tell his father how he wasn't talking because of fear of punishment, not insubordination, and how he wasn't the one making things difficult, his father was. There was so much he wanted to say, yet he knew that he wouldn't do it, at least not yet. He was still too weak and afraid. Maybe when he was older and more physically powerful, but not yet. Not yet at all.

"I beat a kid up," Jacques said, unable to meet his father's gaze. "I got his piss and blood on me. That's what you can see and smell."

"You fucking liar," his father cackled as he grabbed Jacques by the shoulder. "You fucking terrible, horrible liar. I cannot believe that I am even associated with someone as pitiful as you."

Jacques felt nothing when his father said these things. Or at least that's how he wanted to be seen. Inside, there was nothing but turmoil and anger, his father's words part of the reason for their existence. Jacques knew with certainty that no matter what he did, these feelings would never truly disappear, only fade from memory until they were to be recovered for some awful purpose. Maybe the monster was within him. Maybe he was the problem.

His father punched him in the face. Pain exploded across his cheek. A cut that had formed when he had been hit earlier reopened, causing blood to run through his teeth and down his throat. No matter what, though, he wouldn't fall to the ground. He stood up and took it like the man his father so desperately wanted him to be. Maybe his dad would see that he wasn't as weak as he thought if he didn't fall or cry after being struck.

"I fucking hate you, Boy," his father said dismissively. "I cannot express the shame I feel every time I look at you. You come home from school early because you got your shit rocked again, and then you lie to me about it. Why would you not just tell me? Why would you go and lie to me? Your dear, beloved father?"

"I don't know," was all Jacques could muster. He wasn't confident enough to go into detail about all of the fear he held in his heart. He was too scared to be anything but a weak, little maggot.

"Well, you better figure your shit out," his father said. "At this rate, you'll never join me and the boys. You'll never be strong enough to struggle through problems like we can. What you deal with is pussy shit compared to real life out there. We experience true pain that you could never understand. At least not until you become a man. When we bring the demons into heaven, you will only be fodder for their lust, a simple object of their pleasure."

Jacques sprinted through the hall, grinning as the guards chased him. At eighteen, he was one of the youngest members of his father's group. They applauded him for this accolade, even going so far as to say that he was one of their best agents, but Jacques didn't see it. Among his family, he was nothing close to a prodigy, having joined the latest, two years prior. After all, his older brother Hugo was already orchestrating schemes like his father did, and he was still sabotaging the reactors.

He dodged down one hall and then dove into one of the many secret tunnels that the organization had developed over the years. Running from the cops had gotten too easy recently; either Jacques was good at it or the guards had gotten slower and fatter, but whatever the reason, he wasn't complaining.

Pulling himself forward with his elbows, Jacques navigated through the minuscule tunnel. The squeeze was tight, especially for his larger frame. He made it work, though. Nothing would stop him from fulfilling his purpose.

After crawling for quite some time, he emerged out of the hole. As he always did, he took a deep breath, savoring the musty air of their headquarters. It tasted thick and was difficult to breathe; however, it reminded Jacques of some part of his childhood, so he loved it.

He took the stolen file out of his jacket and walked over to the storage room. There, he found the correct category, date, and place for it to be sorted into. The room was monstrous, likely housing tens if not hundreds of thousands of files already. He was just contributing one tiny drop in a massive bucket.

It felt good to be contributing something to society. He had been fortunate that he had been granted entry into the organization or he wouldn't have been nearly as useful. Jacques had always figured that without the help of his family, it was likely that he would have ended up either working in sewage or on the fusion reactors. Both jobs were referred to as noble by the government, but he knew better. They were there so that people could feel useful, contributing extraneous labor for a society that had advanced far enough that humans no longer needed to do those jobs. Just the thought of doing either job made his blood boil.

Jacques checked his watch. His schedule had him training in fifteen minutes. It was a good thing that he had been so good at his job, otherwise, he wouldn't have been able to make it on time.

He ran to his room, changed into his training garb, and then rushed to the gym. Ken and Ramses were already there, bickering. Jacques joined them, happy to be a part of something.

"So then, the guard was trying to taze me, but no matter what he did, he just couldn't hit me!" Ken was saying. "I was jumping around like one of those weird beans, and you could practically smell just how irritated the dude was getting. It was hilarious."

Ramses laughed, but all Jacques could muster was the smallest of half-smiles. He hadn't fully committed to any sort of social emotion in the longest time, and the idea of doing anything but suppressing how he truly felt was foreign to him.

"Those guys are fucking stupid," Ramses added. "One time, I got into a fight with one and tricked him into thinking that he had randomly attacked me for no reason. When he stopped to think about it, I got the hell out, leaving the man struggling to piece his thoughts together."

Ken cackled and what little entertainment that Jacques might have been expressing before disappeared in a flash. He knew that Ramses was lying. None of the guards were that stupid. They were ill-equipped, yes, but they weren't so dumb as to forget what had just happened to them. To say something like that was idiotic.

His father walked into the room, killing all laughter. They turned to him and saluted one-by-one.

"Boys," their father said formally. "Are you excited for a good day of training?"

"Yes, sir," they said in unison.

"Good."

They got on the mat and started warming up. Afterward, they were paired off for training, where they would spar with people in various ways. The first was grappling, which Jacques was particularly good at, then striking, then mixed martial arts, then finally weapons fighting.

All of them were exceptionally good at all of these compared to a normal guard, but within their group, they had people who specialized in each. Of those three, Ken was probably their best striker, Ramses their weapons specialist, and Jacques their grappler. Jacques couldn't have been certain, but he figured that his father had trained that specifically so that they would have diversity in their training. Of course, this idea might have been founded on paranoia and mistrust, so who could have said whether or not it was true?

The only person there who refused to train was his father. Jacques thought him to be weak for this, although he would have never voiced this opinion. The older man was getting fatter with each passing day, and refusing to work out wasn't helping. All of his father's problems only seemed to be compounding due to his sedentary lifestyle.

Afterward, his father took the three of them and a few other people into a room separate from their training area. That was standard. He liked to debrief them on what was going on while checking in on their plans.

Usually, those meetings were relatively light-hearted, full of hope and happiness, but Jacques could see frustration and fear in his father's eyes. Something was wrong.

"Our timeline has been pushed up," he announced.

Ramses cheered stupidly, but at least Ken had the decency to watch the way Jacques and his father reacted to the news before doing anything.

"We don't have enough time," Jacques replied. "Movements take effort and energy, and if we were to ask the public about us right now, nobody would know that we even existed."

"That's the problem, dipshit. We need notoriety. We need prestige. We need to impose our will upon the people in a way that they recognize. Right now, at our current effort levels, we will be relegated to be forgotten in the tides of time. This cannot happen. We must work harder, faster. I suppose that in a sense, our lack of recognition right now is a blessing because it can make our ascension all the more meteoric."

Jacques' lips drew into a line and he nodded slowly. Regardless of how he felt about his father, the things that he was saying were true. They weren't making any real headway with their mission. It was disappointing and needed to change.

"What is going to be different moving forwards, then?"

"That's a perfect segue into my next piece of news," his father said. "The government has just decided who your mate is going to be, Jacques, since you didn't pick one yourself."

Jacques' eyes grew wide. Had he forgotten about that? When was the deadline? His mind raced with thoughts of frustration and regret. He should have been more on top of that, for the organization if not for himself. Spouses could make or break a membership.

"What the fuck?" he whispered. "Is this where my life has led? Is this what my potential is going to be hindered by?"

"If you let it," his father said dismissively. "That's your choice, not mine."

His father went on to talk about all of the things that would be different in the future, but Jacques was embarrassed to admit that he didn't absorb any of the information. He was too busy thinking about the possibility that his wife might report his activities to the government or do something else to stop him from helping the organization. It was terrifying to ponder.

Four men sipped beer around a table at a tavern in the Japanese Sector. They were unaware that Jacques was spying on them, or at least he hoped they were, but even so, a weary hesitance prevailed. It was a common feeling for people throughout *the Dominion of Life*, and he was not the least bit surprised to find that when he sat down to listen, none of them were talking.

It took them a while to warm up to the idea of having casual chit-chat. Jacques was patient though and was glad to have waited, as gradually, a conversation started.

"So what do you guys think?" one of them said, whom Jacques would refer to as Sai.

"About?" a man that Jacques named Hitoro replied. Hitoro was old and serious and seemed to have no problem disputing falsehoods, although those were just Jacques' ignorant first impressions of the man.

"All of the stuff that's been in the news recently," Sai answered. "Doesn't it scare you, just a little bit?"

Nobody replied for some time, and the pervasive fear only appeared to grow stronger. Jacques felt his spirit lift the longer the silence passed over the four men. His father and their organization were doing a good job after all.

Then a much younger man, that Jacques thought of as Katash, was the one to respond. "Who wouldn't be terrified by this? The murder rates are skyrocketing, and the guards haven't done anything to stop it."

"Clearly not," the final man, Rokuro added.

"Is Congressman Tanaka even doing anything about it?" Hitoro asked. "We shouldn't have to live in fear like this."

The observation, however obvious it might have been, was quite astute in Jacques' opinion. They intended to force the people into a state of fear where they would search for hope or an escape. Hope had died many years ago, when the sun had gone out, so the outcome seemed evident to Jacques; they would come to his father and their organization for what the government wasn't providing.

"Tanaka has ignored the Japanese for too long," Rokuro said harshly. "We drink and pretend to enjoy life while he sits in his ivory tower, benefitting from that which hurts his own people."

Sai took a sip and frowned. "The congressman has a lot on his plate. He cannot always be thinking about everyone. He needs to prioritize certain things so anything can get done in the first place."

"Change is coming," Katash said. "It might not be today, and it might not be tomorrow, but soon the people will do something about their problems."

"How, though?" Sai asked. "What the government doesn't control isn't necessary for life, so there is no leverage. We cannot move past this period without more people, and we won't have anything substantial for too long. What could possibly allow us to change?"

Rokuro set his cup down on the table and everyone stopped to look at him. There was something deliberate and cold about his persona, and Jacques was now able to perceive that he was the most highly respected among the four.

"Your concerns are valid," he said. "It is fair to feel as if there is nothing to do, that there is nothing that can be done, but I assure you that that is never the case. Whenever humans are backed into the corner, where they feel as if they can no longer go on, they find a way. That was how we left Earth and made a life here, and that will be how we make a better life for our children. High crime and low quality of life are not new, but they can be ended."

"How?" Sai repeated.

"I've heard people talking about an organization," Rokuro began, and Jacques took a self-satisfied sip. The whispers that they had planted had worked, then. People were beginning to talk. The rumors were placed at strategic places and times so that there was little trust in the guards and high superstition among the citizens.

Happy with how that had gone, Jacques set down his mug and walked out of the tavern. He didn't need to hear them speak any longer to know that within the next few days, they would likely have four new recruits.

-12-

Chief Pedro Girano twiddled his thumbs on the table as he waited for company to arrive. The end was near, far too near for his comfort. Nervousness shrouded him, overcoming his normal mask of stoicism. How far he had fallen to succumb to the will of those that he hated.

He was not foolish enough to be unable to recognize the fact that justice was dying. No matter how much he might have tried to hide it, the very essence of the station was rotten, oozing violence and malice. There was nothing he and his guards could do to stop it, so they tried their best to cover it up, to little to no avail.

Any minute now, the two largest evils he knew of would step into the room and pressure him to act further against his own beliefs. He prepared himself for the threats, the promises, and the plans that would spell the end of everything he held dear.

As if on cue, Tasvas and Monarch Norgaard entered, chatting idly as they joined him at the table. Behind them walked a pair of guards that Girano didn't recognize and a man in a suit that he knew from past meetings but not well enough to remember his name.

"Some people really just have no concept of time," Tasvas said, his large body shaking from the booming of his voice.

Norgaard nodded in agreement. "I cannot stand incompetency." The lines on the old woman's face stretched, and for a moment, Girano wondered if perhaps they would tear under all of the stress.

Nonchalantly, Tasvas placed a box on the table and kept talking. Girano knew well enough at that point to know that it contained some sort of weapon that would immediately kill him if he did anything other than sit and agree with them. He had no idea how it worked, but he knew that he valued his life enough to not try and find out.

They continued to talk about matters that didn't fully concern him, so Girano sat and waited, impatient for the meeting to be over. The man in the suit eyed him coolly every time he looked up from his tablet, although that was infrequent.

Time passed slowly as Girano remained impassive, until finally Tasvas dropped the veil of entertainment and directed his harsh attention to the rest of the table.

"We have been blessed," he grumbled. "With an opportunity at hand, we must strike."

Girano felt his stomach drop. *Strike?* he thought. That could only mean one thing: extinction.

Monarch Norgaard furrowed her brow. "How have we been blessed? What opportunity do you refer to?"

Girano was surprised by this. Had Tasvas not informed her what he was planning to do, specifically? That seemed odd, especially considering how close they appeared to be.

"The details are unimportant," Tasvas replied dismissively. "All you need to know is that you must be vigilant in the coming weeks, awaiting even the smallest command."

Sweat beaded on Girano's forehead. He had much that he wanted to ask but was afraid that he might be shamed, or worse, for speaking. The group was not known for its niceties.

"Spit it out," the cold man in the suit said, seemingly able to see Girano's nervousness. "You have something to say, do you not?"

Girano swallowed. "What do you need us to do?" he asked finally.

"Perfect question," Tasvas said with a devilish smile. He turned to Monarch Norgaard. "First, the powerful and beautiful monarch. All you need to do is turn off all of the alarms and basic electrical systems."

"Why?" she asked.

"You'll see," he responded, his smile broadening to a grin. "And you." His attention was suddenly upon Girano. "Your job is incredibly basic, so fret not. All you have to do is incapacitate the guards."

"Why?" After seeing how Monarch Norgaard and Tasvas were not quite so close, the question felt appropriate for him to ask.

"Conflict is the source of chaos, and chaos is the death of a plan. Order must be maintained at all times."

Girano wasn't sure that he understood the answer but he offered no evidence that this was so or any complaints to the vague response. Instead, he sat and listened, waiting for the meeting to be over. Some time later, he was dismissed and absentmindedly made his way back to his office where he would sit and ponder what he had just learned. Was the fate of the world really left in his cowardly hands?

-13-

Jacques fiddled with his tool belt, his hands shaky and uncertain. Where were the deliberate movements that had served him so well? Where was the surety that he was doing the right thing? *No*, he thought. This is the only way. Regardless of how I feel, I need to follow through with what I have committed to.

Finally, he got everything back where it needed to be. That had taken too long. Clearing his mind to calm himself, he began working on the next steps of their plan. So far, the distractions had been placed, interacting with the guards' communications just long enough for the true event to take place. Now, they just needed to prepare the killing grounds and the artist who would add to the overall effect.

"What the hell are you doing?" Jacques heard from behind him.

Shit. That wasn't how things were supposed to go. "Hey," he said, doing his best not to focus any of his attention on the radio tower that he had just bolted to the ground. "What's up?"

The guard snarled. "What's up? You're acting like you've done nothing wrong. What's wrong with you?"

Jacques' face fell into a familiar state of coldness. He was about to kill the man, he knew. There was no avoiding it. He retrieved his machete from where it hung at his side and swung it around, feeling its weight in his hand.

The guard recoiled slightly upon seeing this. "Stand down," he said, no longer quite so accusatory. "Put the weapon down, and we can talk. I don't want to hurt you."

"I want to hurt you," Jacques countered. "I would very much like to hurt you, in fact."

"Why would you want to hurt me? What have I ever done to you? I'm just trying to do my job. This doesn't have to get violent. If you mess up and I live through this, you'll be sent to the Progenitor of Torment. Do you really want that? None of your loved ones will ever be able to see you again."

"I'm not foolish enough to get caught," Jacques replied.

He jumped towards the guard, unwilling to partake in any further conversation. He hacked at the guard with his machete, drawing blood only after the third swing or so. The guard covered his face with his arms, shouting something that Jacques couldn't understand.

A stabbing pain erupted in his stomach and Jacques looked down to notice a blade embedded in his gut. The guard had struck during Jacques' offensive, likely trying to do some damage before dying. It was valiant, but it wasn't a fatal strike and Jacques forced himself to think of it as nothing but an annoyance for the time being.

He checked his watch. Fuck. There wasn't enough time to clean up the body. His only option was to leave it there and move on. Jacques was getting agitated. Why weren't things working out like he wanted them to? Why was chaos so ever-present that the things that needed to happen couldn't?

The knife's weight hung awkwardly in his stomach. He thought about pulling it out and stopped himself before he could. It was holding his blood in, preventing him from bleeding out until he got the proper medical attention. He was also lucky that his shirt was pretty tight, meaning that it was already applying a minimal amount of pressure to the wound as it was.

Now it was time to perform the next part of the mission. He took a few steps with the knife still in him but it fell out of him, clanging to the ground loudly. It wouldn't have been intelligent or sensible to reach down and put it back in, so Jacques focused on binding the wound. How inconvenient.

Gently, he took off his overshirt, taking care not to pull up the tight undershirt as well. Then, he reached into his tool kit and pulled out a roll of gauze, wrapped it tightly around his torso, and then covered it with his overshirt. It was still bloody. He would have to get a change of clothes or a covering before he went home. He couldn't have his wife asking questions.

Feeling the pain spreading throughout his body, Jacques made his way down the hallway, his walk gradually transforming into a limp as he went. The hair on the back of his neck prickled up as if he were being watched. Frantically, he searched to see if his instincts were failing him, eventually falling back into his limp after understanding that the pain of getting stabbed was just getting to be too much to properly control.

He trudged along, eventually arriving at his destination. The scene of the massacre was admittedly not as brutal as he had imagined. Had he been working as a direct killer, as he had wanted, there would have been more ruthlessness and death by a large margin. It was disappointing that they had only forced 12 guards to their deaths and not more. Would that even make the news? Who would follow a movement that nobody knew about?

Nobody had even painted the message yet. Jacques couldn't believe how unprofessional the organization was becoming. Where were the coordinated efforts for the usurpation of a regime that had been built upon false moral codes? It was beginning to feel like they were just common criminals.

Fortunately, Jacques had packed a paintbrush for that exact

occasion. He wiped the bristles in the guts of one of the dead guards, whose head was now on a spike, and started to paint. He wasn't known for his artistry, but it was better than nothing. The words would only serve to add to the overall aesthetic of the scene.

It didn't take him very long and soon after he had finished, he put his brush away and moved down the hall in the direction of headquarters. The lights in the corridor had been put out by his colleagues, leaving him to navigate through the darkness. It was a good thing that he had been taught to do so years ago when he had joined the organization so he had no trouble whatsoever.

He reached an intersection, and upon a whim, he looked down the hall to his right. There were lights on in the distance, illuminating a short figure. Jacques wasn't sure how, but he got the feeling he knew who that it was. "Juliette?" he whispered, praying to anyone who would listen that she wouldn't turn and see him. What if she recognized him and followed? What if she discovered what was going on? He couldn't allow that. At that moment, he resolved to kill her if such an eventuality came to fruition.

Her figure grew smaller, though, and Jacques knew that he wouldn't need to resort to such actions. He thought back through what had just happened and had a vague memory of the hour being announced. How long ago had that been? He wasn't wearing a watch and had no real concept of time, especially not when he was doing a job. It was one of his weaknesses as an agent for the organization.

Quickly and without thought, he went back to headquarters, changed, ditching his tools in the process, and then limped his way to his death trap of a home. At some point during his journey back, it occurred to him that changing might have been a silly thing to do, especially since she would have been able to see him shirtless anyways. No matter. There was nothing he could do about it anymore.

Their house came into view, and Jacques felt a sort of bile rise in his throat. As with every other time he saw his wife, he thought about how he should have registered for a different spouse, more specifically one that was an active supporter of his father's organization. Instead, he had been stuck with a simple, small, unattractive woman who was interested in Jacques being someone that he wasn't.

Hesitation was the vice of those who lost, so Jacques swallowed his anxieties and frustrations and stepped through the door. In his heart, he held hope that he might be alone, that she had gone to her parents for the night, but his dreams were immediately dashed. In the kitchen she stood, her expression telling him that she was expecting some grandiose gesture from him.

"Welcome home," she said far too enthusiastically. "Roast beef is in the oven and should be done soon."

He groaned, refusing to acknowledge her as he went and dropped his things into their room. Jacques felt a pit of frustration open in his gut, which only grew when he tried to remind herself that he shouldn't care. He had just done so much work for the organization, and as far as he was concerned, she was the death of his efforts.

Deliriously, he looked through the master bedroom to see if there was anything that he needed, remembering part-way through his search that he was wounded. The bathroom was his next destination, containing all of the gauze, water, and antiseptics that he might need.

He looked over his shoulder to see Juliette standing in the doorway, worry and irritation plastered on her face. "Hey," he said uncomfortably. He wished she would just leave him alone.

"Hey," Juliette replied, far less enthusiastically than he had been expecting. Perhaps she wasn't so dense that she couldn't take hints, then.

"It's dangerous out there," he said as he examined himself, trying to fill the void with something other than his pained grunts. He might have hated her, but he hated socially awkward situations too. "Things get out of hand, and people get hurt."

"I see that," she responded, clearly trying to indicate that she was upset. Jacques prepared himself for the inevitable outburst that he would do nothing to stop. That was her decision, not his.

He peeled off his undershirt with the bandage still wrapped around it and blood immediately started to flow down his pants. A stabbing pain attacked him for a few seconds, robbing him of his ability to form coherent thoughts. Soon, the sensation faded, and he was able to see that the wound had reopened after taking off his shirt; apparently, the scab had grown into the fabric. Stoically, he took the gauze and started to wrap it around his body. It felt good to have the area covered up again and not bleeding all over him.

Juliette ducked out of the doorway where her mood had obviously changed from nervousness to anger. Had Jacques cared, he would have called out to her and asked her to help him with his bloody clothes, but he didn't so he didn't. Instead, he balled them up and threw them into the bath. He would clean them with bleach later. Now was the time for his wound to be tended to.

It was then that he realized that in his bloodless daze, he had forgotten to use the antiseptics. Unwilling to take off the gauze that had already been wrapped perfectly, he took the rubbing alcohol and poured it over the wound. It hurt so much that he thought he was going to die. He started to shake uncontrollably, but his will was strong enough that he remained silent through it all.

It took a few seconds of some of the deepest breathing Jacques had ever done for him to feel calm and composed once more. That was good enough for the time being. Juliette had spent all of that time making roast beef for him, and as much as he hated her, he loved the meal, so he would do it the courtesy of eating it. In his bedroom, he found a change of clothes and then returned to the kitchen to eat.

Filled with the savory scents of gravy and meat, the kitchen reminded Jacques of just how hungry he was and how long it had been since he had eaten a real meal. To keep a low profile, his father always preferred that they consumed calorie pills instead of eating real food. He said that it minimized waste, which Jacques figured was the truth. It just would have been nice to eat something satisfying every once in a while.

Angrily, Juliette slammed the roast beef on the table in front of him, then went and added the gravy to the ensemble. He looked around, wondering where his utensils would be, deciding that he would just use his hands if she didn't bring him any, when she brought a knife and fork to him as well.

He dug in happily, cutting off pieces of meat and dipping them into the gravy. It was so succulent and tender that Jacques practically fainted from the taste. It was easily the most delicious thing that he had ever eaten. She might have been a pain in his ass, but she sure as hell knew how to cook.

"That's it?" She shrieked, piercing Jacques' peace. "I make you a nice meal and this is how you treat me? No 'thank you,' or even 'this looks delicious?!' You are always so unbelievably rude."

Calmly, Jacques set his knife down on the table. "You know my feelings towards you," he said. "You weren't even my third choice. I don't hate you, nor do I feel any malevolence towards you." This was a lie, although she didn't need to know that. "Instead, I pity myself that I got stuck with you and wonder if life could have been different if I would have been able to learn about love. Instead, I got stuck with you. I don't hate or seethe, I simply wish that things would have been different."

Juliette grabbed her coat from the pitiful chair that had likely never been used. She was about to leave, so it was important that he finish what he was saying.

"I hope you take solace in the fact that I have never hated you. I am only this cold around you because you are not the one for me, and I know I could never possibly feel any sort of love towards you."

She rushed out the door, but he was too busy eating to pay any attention to her feelings. She was the kind of creature that cared far more about relationships than she should. People were a means to an end, not a source of happiness. It was naive of her to think anything less.

Jacques walked through the rainforest, slightly sad that it would be his fate to destroy it. Everything was so green and beautiful, completely unlike the way that the rest of the unnatural ship was. Perhaps if he had been born in a different time, a time when Earth was still alive, he would have been given the option to enjoy such things.

His companion, Ferdinand, was feeling the same way. His scarred face radiated regret and shame. Furious at himself for experiencing weakness akin to that of his teammates, Jacques put on a stoic mask and busied himself by triple-checking the blastshrooms. They had been systematically planted over the course of the past four years and according to their data, they were currently at a critical population. The next steps in their plans were becoming a reality. This realization was even more beautiful to Jacques than the forest.

"Maybe we should wait," Ferdinand suggested. "It would

work better if we had more blastshrooms to work with. We have no guarantee that all of their flammable spores will be released correctly, after all."

Jacques whipped around, grinning darkly at Ferdinand. "You want to stop, don't you? You want to abandon everything just because you saw some pretty flowers."

"No, man," Ferdinand said, backtracking. "I just want to make sure we've thought of everything before we do something this drastic. Have we thought about the effects of this and how it will influence the people? Maybe we should do something else."

Jacques advanced on the man, pulling his machete out of its sheath. "Don't give me a reason to make you join them," he said, motioning to the guards that they had tied to a nearby tree. One of them struggled against his restraints, yelling into his gag, while the others were still unconscious.

"You can't kill me," Ferdinand said, although it was evident that he didn't believe the words he was saying. "Your father values my experience and skills as well, not just yours. Let me speak without threatening my life, please."

Jacques snarled and leaped towards the man, fully ready to chop his head off when his brother Hugo came into the clearing. "What's going on?" the small, quiet man asked. "Why are you trying to kill our peer?"

The judgment behind his words hit Jacques harder than he would have liked to admit. "He wasn't committed to our cause," he responded to Hugo. "He wanted to delay because he has forgotten the reason that we do this."

"Then perhaps you should have reeducated him," Hugo said dismissively, focusing more on the tablet in his hand than their current conversation. "Murder is not the only solution for these things."

Jacques went quiet, unsure how he was supposed to retaliate, if at all. His hand quivered, urging him onwards to kill the other man. Oh, how he hated it when his violent delights were interrupted. It ruined his day. Now he would have to find something else to kill if he were to feel fully sane.

"Combustion is scheduled to happen in the next 70 seconds," Hugo explained. "We need to leave. Now"

Jacques wanted to stay to hack one of the guards to pieces, but he knew his brother wouldn't allow it. While Hugo was physically weak, his mind was quite strong. On top of that, Jacques would be reported to his father for insubordination, and he didn't want to deal with that.

As they turned to leave, Jacques heard splashing in a nearby creek. Somebody else was there. Maybe he could murder them instead? He would have to do it when his brother wasn't watching, but that might work in his favor. If he could catch the person off-guard, then he could watch them struggle as he ripped them to pieces. Perfect.

He came over a small hill and the person came into view. Jacques' heart dropped. Juliette. Why was she there? It was so inconvenient. He had been so happy about the prospect of satisfying his blood lust before and just like that, his dreams had been dashed. She was very good at doing that, it seemed.

As with every other time he had pondered killing her, the reptilian part of his mind considered how easy it would have been to rush down, end her life, and rush away as if nothing had happened. Unfortunately for him, though, the long-term and more sophisticated part of his conscience reminded him that his father had forbidden him from killing his wife and that he was stuck with her.

She stepped out of the water, and he saw that she was covered in blastshroom spores. *No*, he thought. If the flames reached her, she would be killed immediately. The spores were essentially made of gunpowder, exploding when heated to a certain temperature.

Suddenly, the world around him was transformed into a hellscape of fire and booms. Luckily for him, they were still a few seconds away. He still had time to run and save her. His feet carried him before his mind could react, not giving him any time to ask himself why he was saving her. It made sense to just leave her there and allow nature to take hold of her, but something inside of him hated the idea of that.

He grabbed her after she tripped and carried her towards the exit. She fell limp in his arms, likely unconscious. Running was slower with her but not impossible. Ash fell onto his face, trees collapsed, and he knew that the fire was catching up to him. It was his fault, he supposed; he had been a huge proponent for using more spores rather than less.

Flames nipped at his heels and adrenaline pushed him forwards, faster than he could have imagined. It might have just been deliria from the smoke, but he felt like he was a ship whose sails were full of wind. The world passed by in a blur, and before he knew it, he was outside of the forest.

Jacques watched on as the fires of hell tore down the grandeur of nature. The heat grew with each passing moment, making it unbearable to watch after just a few seconds. He turned to leave, only stopping when he was reminded of Juliette on his back. If she hadn't been with him, he wouldn't have been so close to the fire and he would have been able to watch it longer. It infuriated him that she was always there to drag him down.

Nonchalantly, he took her off his back and threw her into the fire. If she deserved to die, they would claim her and there would be nothing he could do about it. However, if she was strong enough and deserved to live, she wouldn't let something like that claim her life as its own.

Her body remained motionless as the flames approached. Jacques silently prayed that they would envelop her and take her from him. How perfectly clean that would be, to live without her. And he wouldn't have killed her, either. The fires would have. Everything was falling into place, and he could not have been happier about it.

But the heat combustion never reached her. It got close, yes, perhaps within 10 or 20 feet; however, this wasn't enough to kill her. Agitated by this development, Jacques ran to the fire and retrieved a stick that was mostly cool except for one end that was on fire. If it wouldn't go to her of its own volition, then he would bring it to her.

Biting down hard with anger, Jacques clenched the stick tightly and jammed it into Juliette's stomach. It would hardly suffice for what he had wanted in terms of damage, but it was better than nothing.

After a while, perhaps a minute, maybe more, he noticed that the stick was no longer burning. He would have preferred that it would have burned longer, of course, although that amount of time wasn't too terrible.

Something inside him suddenly felt wrong. *Why am I doing this?* he thought, although he knew the answer. It was because he wanted to. However, no matter how much he tried to convince himself of that fact, he couldn't get over the internal conflict.

She doesn't deserve this.

No. She does, she stole my life.

She didn't mean to.

It doesn't matter what she meant.

It does.

The result is the only thing that matters.

Her feelings do, too.

Hatefully, Jacques picked the burnt Juliette off of the ashy forest floor and put her on his shoulder. His kindness had won this time. No longer did he feel so energetic that he could traverse the station without expending much effort, and he quickly found that even just a little over a hundred pounds could quickly become quite burdensome.

With heavy legs and a foggy mind, he found himself setting her in her bed some time later. The smoke had gotten to him. His lungs hurt from burning and exertion. Next time, if there was a next time, he would make sure to wear a mask. Escape had taken far too long. He should have predicted that something might come up to stop him from making it out on time.

Fatigued and unlikely to admit that he was terrified of how he was feeling, Jacques sat on the bedroom floor and permitted himself to rest, if only briefly. He knew he needed to leave before she awoke. She couldn't see him like that. On top of that, he had told her that he would be on a mining trip for the next week or so, so his presence would have been suspicious either way.

Tiredness washed over him, though, and before he knew it, he was nodding off, imagining fantastical things waiting in the shadows for him. After all, he knew that there weren't any men with white hair and eyes waiting in the shadows to approach him about an important topic of conversation. And the hand that felt so real resting on his shoulder couldn't have been there. He had checked beforehand. He was alone.

Jacques blinked and found that he was not alone. There was the man with white hair and eyes, sitting casually next to him on the ground. There was something familiar about the stranger, something that Jacques couldn't quite get a handle on. He knew better than to open up fully, though, and told himself that he would be careful.

"Jacques Lavigne," the stranger started. His voice was smooth and comfortable, forcing the skepticism out of Jacques' mind. He could trust the other man.

"Hello," he replied. "Have we met before?"

"Many times," the man said with a nod, "although I'm certain you cannot remember any of them."

"Why not?"

"You were of a different mind then, I suppose. Memories don't always transcend like we need them to."

Jacques had no idea what the stranger was talking about. Perhaps he was just crazy.

"I am many things, but I am not crazy," the man told him. "Well, at least I don't think I am. Although a crazy person would think that, wouldn't they. What do you think?"

"Are you crazy?"

"Or is there any way for a crazy person to be able to self-diagnose their ailment?"

Jacques thought for a moment. Why was he so interested in answering? It shouldn't have mattered to him in the slightest. Philosophy was for people who were too weak to find conviction within violence.

"Perhaps if they become self-aware enough to recognize the actions of their peers?" he replied with uncertainty.

The stranger grunted and nodded. "I think I like that idea. It makes sense to me."

Jacques frowned, knowing full well that he was in the middle of one of the strangest interactions he had ever had in his life.

"Anyways," the stranger said abruptly, "that's not why I've come to speak with you."

"It's not?" Jacques hadn't even realized that there had been a purpose behind the conversation. It felt far too chaotic for a typical direction to be found.

"Not in the slightest, my child. You truly are remarkable. Where the rest of humanity failed, you have succeeded. In the process, you have become an agent of death, which I would be inclined to refer to as a good thing."

Jacques grinned. "An agent of death?" He loved the sound

of that. "And how have I succeeded?"

"You discovered true power within the fire," the man said nonchalantly. "You found it as few others have. I must say, I was not merely surprised by this but also impressed."

Jacques blinked in understanding. Everything was starting to make so much more sense. "Are you God?"

The man laughed. "Some might say so. I would not."

"Why not?"

"Because I am not talking to you to give you advice but rather to ask for it. What kind of god confers with mortals?"

"That makes sense," Jacques admitted, slightly disappointed. A part of him was hoping that he had finally met the divine being that he served so lovingly. Perhaps this was just a stranger after all, then.

"Explain your thoughts on death for me, then," the man said.

"My thoughts on death? In what way?"

"How to avoid it, how to enforce it, how to enjoy it when it is the final option." The man shrugged. "I just want to hear what you think. Anything could help."

Jacques took a moment to organize his ideas. There was so much he could say in response, and so much that felt important for the man to know, that he wasn't sure where to begin. Should he start with how good it felt to murder someone, or how the permanence of death reinforced the strength and import of life?

"It is the only thing of true permanence, after all," the man continued, guiding Jacques' thought process.

"The permanence has significance, though," Jacques replied. "If it were so simple as going to sleep, only to wake up again, it would not be nearly as satisfying or scary. To me, it is a means to an end that I have come to enjoy. To others, it is the worst thing that could ever happen."

"And it isn't the worst thing that could ever happen to you?"

the man asked with a raised eyebrow. "Whyever not?"

"Because I know pain," Jacques answered. "Death might be the end, but it is also relief. Perhaps if you are so terrified of the end, think about all of the terrible things that are ending with it."

Jacques' eyes drooped slowly. How was he that tired already? Hadn't he just awoken from a nap, only to have a short conversation? What had made him feel that way?

"Thank you," the man said, his words breaking through the veil of fatigue. "You are wise beyond your understanding."

Jacques shot to his feet. *Where am I?* he thought, panicking. The room was initially dark but was gradually brightening as he adjusted to his surroundings. He was still in Juliette's room. But that couldn't be. That conversation had felt so real. It had to have happened. He had never had a dream that lucid. He held his head in frustrated confusion. Nothing made sense.

Being pushed on by either insanity or sympathy, he moved to check on Juliette. Maybe he just needed some time to let his mind clear. Maybe it had just been a dream after all. Maybe he could talk to her about it. She had always seemed so kind and available, after all.

Suddenly, she stirred, and all thoughts of staying leapt from his mind. He had to leave, to run, to get someplace where he could truly be alone with his thoughts. He had things that he needed to figure out.

Juliette moved again. She was definitely awake now. Her breathing had become less rhythmic and even as it was when she had been asleep. "Mom?" she asked, and Jacques wasted no more time, bolting to the front door.

As he ran away from her, his lungs burned and tears streamed down his face. It was from the fire, of course. He couldn't have been crying from something so simple as emotion. There was nothing that could shake him so much that he would run away from someone that could help, crying. It was from the fire, of course. It couldn't have been the fact that he no longer felt at home in his head, terrified that he had started to hallucinate. It was from the fire, of course.

It had been 24 hours and Jacques still hadn't left headquarters. No one had questioned his reasoning behind that decision, luckily, as they had all bought his explanation that had involved the fire and the detrimental effects it had had on him.

Well, no one besides Hugo had questioned him. With frustration, Jacques thought of how accusatory and skeptical his older brother had been about the situation. He kept bouncing between how Jacques was either stupid or lying because they had planned for enough escape time. Jacques was too proud to admit that he had stayed behind to save his wife and too intelligent to tell anyone why. So he was stuck, unable to tell anyone how conflicted and afraid he felt.

He felt a buzzing in his pocket and pulled his tablet out. Ferdinand was calling. Jacques thought about swiping down and ignoring it, although he knew that he would never actually do it. His father was not so lenient that he would allow direct disregard for duty like that. So, reluctantly, Jacques answered.

His scar-faced comrade was standing in the dark. Jacques opened his mouth to say something, but there was something about the demeanor of Ferdinand that told him that that would have been a bad idea. Something was up. Suddenly, being on call didn't seem like such a good decision. Without a word and hoping that he was making the right choice, Jacques hung up. If his intuition was right, he had just saved their entire mission, and if he was wrong, he had just pissed off a lot of people. Only time would tell.

Although something was telling him that his intuition would hardly be wrong anymore.

Of all of the things that Jacques hated in life, helping his dad on the Progenitor of Torment had to be the worst. There was absolutely nothing redeeming about the experience; he could only watch torture and not participate in it, all the while cleaning and helping with management. It was like locking a coke addict to a chair and allowing him to stare at his next fix but not allowing him to get to it.

Every time he visited, Jacques felt something tickling the inside of his body, urging him toward the bullet-proof cells that housed the inmates. And every time, he asked himself if it would be worth it to break in and torture and kill one of the prisoners. The rational part of him told him, no, but the longer he stayed, the harder it was to convince himself that that was the truth.

Presently, his father, who was either playing the part of a warden or was the warden, was awaiting the arrival of some diplomatic leader from *the Dominion of Life*. According to his sources, she would be arriving within the next 5 minutes or so.

"Is she not too busy to visit?" Ramses asked nervously. "Isn't Congress in session?"

"No," Father replied. "This is right at the beginning of their break period."

Jacques sighed and rolled his eyes. Ramses was nothing if not a moron. He rarely paid attention during briefings, and even when he did, it seemed that he had little to no understanding of what had just been presented. Jacques had to wonder why someone like that was so well-liked by his father. It was befuddling, and he doubted that he would ever truly understand the answer.

A void of noise surrounded them naturally, for Jacques knew that his father wouldn't allow any further discussion. They had a job coming up, or rather, a mission. Nothing less than absolute focus was expected.

His hands shook, and whether it was from a craving for blood or from nervousness, Jacques wasn't sure. He heard footsteps in the hall leading up to the waiting room, their volume increasing with the tempo of his heart.

And finally, at the peak of the brilliant crescendo, Ebuka Abdullahi, the core of their plot to save the world from itself, stepped through the threshold, her eyes conveying nothing but disdain and fury.

"Who are you here to see today?" his father asked, putting on a voice. It had been hard enough to fit him into the fat suit that Jacques wondered if that part of the disguise would have been adequate, but he insisted that it wouldn't. It was better to be safe than to fail, Jacques supposed.

"Just go get him," Ebuka said curtly. Jacques blinked in surprise, regretting it immediately after with hope that she hadn't noticed. They hadn't given her any reason to be rude, had they?

"I'm afraid I cannot go get him since I do not know who you mean," his father replied, both entertained and confused. The interaction was already so strange that Jacques wondered if perhaps only odd people could become members of Congress.

The crazy woman that seemed to think she was smarter than she was stomped over to his father and attempted an extremely poorly executed shirt grab. Was she trying to intimidate his father? Jacques wanted to laugh; it was just too much. He, who had been referred to as an agent of death, was still unable to intimidate his father. How the hell did she expect to do anything even remotely along those lines?

"What?" she spat. "Do you want me to destroy myself by saying this to you? Do you truly believe that there is something about admitting that my father is in prison that has any impact on how I view myself? You are an embarrassment. If I were your mother I would have killed myself because of how little my efforts to accomplish anything mattered. Fuck you."

Now Jacques was thoroughly confused. Quietly, he walked himself through the situation to ensure that he hadn't missed anything. Firstly, she had arrived with a sour disposition. Secondly, she had verbally and physically attacked his father. There didn't seem to be any connection to Jacques, so he just assumed that she was dealing with stress. He had found that often when people didn't know why they did certain things, they blamed it on stress. It felt oddly convenient, but who was he to argue with the only rational explanation to an incredibly irrational situation.

"That's it?" his father asked. Jacques could hear the amusement in his tone. "How disappointing. I expected more from you, Ebuka Abdullahi. You march in with hatred in every aspect of your being, and that's all you could muster? I have heard stories of your legendary will to do good and was expecting something of that sort, not of an adolescent attempting to hurl insults across the playground. Perhaps next time you will be more prepared."

"Just go get my father so I can get out of this shithole faster," she snarled, and for a moment, Jacques thought that she would wind up and punch him. Part of him wanted to, as he knew his father would allow him to kill her then. Unfortunately, she was not so irrational and released his shirt from her grasp.

It took him a moment to realize what she had just said. *Father?* he thought. Why was her father in prison? He assumed his father had the answer to that question, and that likely was the reason that they had picked to meet with her; he just wasn't privy to any of that information. Not that it mattered, though, as his father had everything under control.

"I will have one of my people do it," his father replied calmly. "In the meantime, I would love to keep talking to you."

Ebuka's frown deepened, which Jacques hadn't realized was possible before he had seen it, and her silence remained. Her behavior was flabbergasting. Nothing about the way that she was acting made sense to him. If he could read her mind, or even just her character, he would have loved to, if only to understand the situation he was in.

Something tickled his mind, almost as if to say that he could if he wanted to.

"I remember the first time your father broke," his father started. Jacques felt his confusion start to fade to excitement. He loved it when his father emotionally ruined people. It was incredibly satisfying. "It was magnificent. His heart carried memories from an irrecoverable time, and with his sanity, those too faded. I am grateful that I was blessed enough to witness something like that."

When Ebuka closed her eyes and started to take deep breaths, Jacques knew that his father had already won. Where contests of the body might have been his specialty, contests of the mind were his father's. And it was terrifyingly fascinating how effective he could be at times.

Jacques heard a noise come from behind him and turned to see Ferdinand and Ken escorting a large Nigerian man into the room. He was extraordinarily bulky, and suddenly, Jacques didn't feel quite so confident in his status as an agent of death. It seemed almost certain that if he were to get into a physical altercation with her father, he would be killed without difficulty. Not for the first time in a few days, Jacques vacated his mind briefly, collapsing in on himself as he felt his Identity weaken to the point that it was unable to support him any longer.

But then she opened her mouth to speak, and Jacques' curiosity was enough to bring him back into the moment. Maybe he could glean more information on the reasoning behind her actions by listening in?

"How are you?" Ebuka asked, suddenly far less angry.

The man whom she called father did not appear to be quite so lucid that he could respond to her question, or even talk for that matter. Looking into his eyes, Jacques saw neither affection nor recognition. This was a vacant soul, one of the people that were the most far gone in the Progenitor. Jacques had often asked his father if he could torture and kill one of the vacant souls, but his father had always refused, for some reason.

"Do you know who I am?" Ebuka asked, clearly unable to let go of her last bits of hope.

"I- I have had a lot of time to think," the man replied, far more concentrated than he should have been. "I have been granted an eternity, gifted it for the purpose of discovering something." There it was. Jacques had been concerned that he had completely misread the situation. "I feel that I am on the verge of knowing what my purpose is; I just need to spend more time in solitude to figure it out. They must send me back. I've already spoken to you for too long."

Jacques' heart skipped a beat when the monster of a man rose to his feet to leave. Could they reasonably stop him without killing him? He thought not. Crazy people were already scary, and strength was another beast to be factored into the equation. Simply put, Jacques was sure that he was staring at one of the most dangerous people in the history of *the Dominion of Life*, perhaps even ever.

"Do you remember your name, inmate?" Ebuka said.

Inmate? Jacques thought. Wasn't he her father? Why the hell was she acting so weird?

"I can't stay!" the monstrous man shrieked. On instinct, Jacques' hand jumped to the taser at his side. There was about to be a big problem. "My cell cannot remain empty for this long! It requires me to be there for me to be alive!"

Ebuka stupidly reached out to the wild beast and placed her hand on his. "You will be perfectly fine. We suspended those systems so that you could talk to me. I needed to talk to you because your mind has advanced so much. You are our only hope."

Jacques was expecting the man to lose his mind and rage, to break everyone and everything around him with a fury that had never been seen before, but instead, some of his sanity returned "I am?"

What the hell? Jacques turned to look at his father, who had never truly left the room. What was that look on his face? Had he known that something like that would happen, or was it simply a step that had to be taken in their plans? For the first time in a long time, Jacques felt himself growing angry that his father had withheld information from them. All of their lives were on the line because of the monstrous man; it would have been helpful and intelligent for his father to have briefed them on his plans.

"Yes, you are. Your purpose, which I am sure you have already figured out, is to answer a series of questions."

He nodded intently. "Yes, that's it, exactly.

"I have come with the questions. Are you ready to fulfill your reason for living?"

He nodded again, his insanity likely the fuel for his irrationality. Why was he believing the things that she was saying? It was absurd.

"I should add that this is only one minuscule part of your purpose. The beginning, I suppose. So prepare yourself for all of the greatness that is to come after." Jacques stifled a groan. She was manipulating him incredibly well. Where had she learned to do something like that? Congresspeople were supposed to be honest and virtuous, weren't they?

"Well obviously," her father said as if that made any sense.

"That book that you took from your daughter's eighth

birthday party, what was it and why did you take it from her?"

Jacques frowned. Why was she asking about something so trivial as that? Was she trying to execute some sort of brainwashing?

"How am I supposed to remember?..." He froze, recognition flashing across his face. "Wait. Maybe I know what you mean. Are you talking about Ebuka? Or? I need to think. What book could you possibly mean?"

"You know," she replied, although Jacques was fairly certain that he did not. He was one of the vacant souls. They didn't remember or truly know anything.

"I don't!" he cried, only proving Jacques right. The conversation was futile; nothing productive would come of it.

Perhaps he should step in and break them apart under the guise of needing to keep her father safe? She was an idiot if she thought that she could do anything other than waste her time. It was aggravating to watch; he would never make a mistake so egregious as that. In the end, the only thing stopping him from doing just that was his father, who he knew would not approve of such action. A moment appeared to pass between the two of them, and not for the first time in his life, he wished he could read people better.

"The only thing that I can think of is a book called 'The Falseness of the Final Flicker,'" her father said.

Jacques' eyes widened as time froze. What had he just said? The Falseness of the Final Flicker? She was targeting them and she didn't even realize it! *Holy fuck*, he thought. How had she found that book? How had she remembered that? He was fairly certain that they had erased all existence of it from the archives and taken care of anyone with a copy. Where was this crack in their plans coming from? Time reverted to normal, but his understanding of the scenario was still quite skewed.

"My mind is not what it once was. I apologize for my incompetence."

Jacques could not even begin to fathom what was going on in her father's head. He looked at his father and saw nothing but impassiveness. How was he reacting so coolly to this discovery? Wasn't it catastrophic? It's just part of his plan, Jacques convinced himself after moments of confusion.

"Where would I be able to find that book?" she asked. "Would you still have one in your possession, or would it be located elsewhere?"

"I keep it safe," her father replied. "I can't have Ebuka finding it. She can't get involved. She's too young. She's far too young for something like that. I can't have her getting involved. She's far too young for something like that. I can't have her getting involved. She's far too young for something like that. I can't have her getting involved. She's far too young for something like that. I can't have her getting involved."

Her father seemed to be stuck on those sentences, as he continued to repeat them for some time. Ebuka, on the other hand, had fallen silent and refused to speak. Why was she not happier? Hadn't she just figured out what she needed?

She waved with her hand for Ferdinand and Ken to take her father away, and Jacques silently cheered, glad that he didn't need to deal with either of them any longer.

"No!" the large man shrieked as they pulled him away from her. "Don't take me! I still have more to give, more to do! My thoughts aren't enough anymore! I need to act!"

Ebuka stood in a vigilant silence, watching with care as her father was taken back to his torturous cell. It was something that Jacques could never understand. If his father were to be taken away like that, Jacques was fairly certain that he would have just felt pity and disdain. Imprisonment, be it from society or an actual prison, was weakness.

She turned to the opposite direction of her father and left

them alone in the room. How foolish.

Suddenly, his father changed from a still creature to an animated leader. "Quickly, we must act," he said. "I am currently sending her pod back to *the Dominion*, where it will act as a message to our comrades that it is time for everything to begin."

A realization dawned on Jacques. Was his father truly planning for Ragnarok to take place that day? Why so soon? Were they ready yet? Jacques felt his breath quicken. They weren't prepared.

"Invasion?" Hugo asked from behind all of them, getting a jump out of Jacques.

"Invasion," his father confirmed. "Turn your headsets on. We need to be prepared for anything."

Static rang through Jacques' ears for a moment, and then she spoke.

"I'm ready to go," she called into their ears. From her perspective, she was just shouting into the emptiness of the hall with nobody near her to listen. Jacques was becoming increasingly certain that she was insane.

By design, none of them responded. They were simply listening, hoping for the variables to perfectly align and bring about the best possible outcome.

"Hello?"

Jacques looked to his father expectedly. The older man's gaze seemed to say 'almost.'

The very air stood still as they passed the time. She was likely in the process of discovering her mistake.

"It's time," his father announced suddenly. "Prepare yourselves. This is what we have been working towards. Momentarily, we will be known. If we are careful, this will be the most natural send-off into the afterlife that humanity could have received. If we are careless, it will be our doom. Watch closely either way, though. This is what happens when heaven falls."

Suddenly, a deafening alarm blared, making Jacques jump just a little. ESCAPE ATTEMPT, it screamed. ESCAPE AT-TEMPT. LOCKDOWN PROTOCOL ACTIVATED.

His father pressed a button, and the dark speech signify-ing Ragnarok began. "Ebuka Abdullahi, defeated by a simple warden," his father declared. "So sad to see. Perhaps here, you and your father can be broken together. What a concept, being reunited with him. I would very much like to see that. How un-fortunate it is that Ragnarok approaches."

WHEN HEAVEN FALLS

-1-

The first thing that Juliette noticed wasn't how she was just slightly lighter, or how the world outside the station was rising; it was how a magnetic levitator on Ebuka's desk started to rise higher than normal. The difference was imperceptibly different, to the point that she was surprised that she had noticed them in the first place, but there it was.

Tim's reaction, which was one of genuine fear and panic, all but confirmed her suspicions. Something was wrong. Well, that seemed obvious. It was just that she wasn't well-versed enough in the physics of the station to be able to explain what exactly was happening.

"You're a maintenance worker, yes?" Tim said, more as a statement than a question.

Juliette nodded.

"Would you be so kind as to take us to an operations panel? Or just present the data to us?"

"Of course," she replied.

Cautiously, she led them out of Ebuka's office and into the hall where she could access one of the panels. She retrieved her key from her pocket and unlocked the small compartment, revealing the tablet that was embedded in the wall.

"What would you like to know?" she asked.

"Does it say anything immediately? Is anything flashing across the screen, like an error message?"

Juliette frowned. "No, it's completely normal. Should it be saying something more?"

Tim furrowed his eyebrows. "This could either be really good or really bad," he said. "I cannot tell you which one, though."

Juliette groaned. She was growing tired of Tim. His attitude was depressingly arrogant as if he despised the fact that he knew that he was above everyone else. She wished he would just shut up and act normal.

"What is happening?" she asked begrudgingly.

"The ship's orbit is decaying," Tim said as he looked out the window. "That's why everything feels lighter, and the world around us appears to be ascending. Someone has sabotaged the propulsive systems aboard this station, and we are now descending towards Jupiter."

"The control panel would tell me if that were true," she replied skeptically. Something about him was making it very hard for her to trust what he was saying, especially when he was spouting nonsense like that. As a maintenance worker, she knew how sensitive the systems aboard *the Dominion* were. Whenever even the slightest imbalance in air composition occurred, she got an alert and an error message, and a decaying orbit like he mentioned was far more catastrophic.

"Not if that were sabotaged as well," he explained. "It seems highly probable that this is related to Ragnarok."

Juliette said nothing as she had nothing to say. She had no way to know if what he was saying were true; all she could do was watch and hope that nothing too terrible happened. So they returned to Ebuka's office and sat down. This new development was out of the realm of their control.

"We should contact somebody," Tim announced after a few moments without conversation.

Juliette felt something familiar growing in her chest. She couldn't describe what it was exactly, although she knew that there was a tension inside of her and she needed to release it somehow.

"I'll call Ebuka, and she can tell you what to do. She is quite good at these things."

Juliette took deep breaths, knowing that a release would mean peace, but fear kept her from approaching the edge of her emotions.

"What do you think?" he asked.

"I think that you're wasting my time," Juliette snapped. "I think you're an asshole. I think you have no idea who you are or what you're doing, and you are hiding under a veil of arrogance."

The corner of Tim's mouth turned up. "Fair enough," he said. "I will remain quiet, then."

Juliette turned away from him to watch the world rise around them. Was the station actually falling? Was that even possible? How could that make any sense? Was there anything elaborate enough to be able to defeat all of the fail-safes that had been put in place? She stole a glance at Tim and saw nothing but seriousness plastered across his face. She found it aggravating that a part of her cared what he thought. He could have just been lying to her that entire time for all she knew. There was no proof behind any of his words. Her father certainly had not been a terrorist sympathizer.

Suddenly, the world stopped in place and Juliette felt normal again. "Our orbit decayed to a point," Tim said, more likely to himself than to anyone else. "But what could it mean? Why here? What was the reason behind doing that? Shouldn't they have just let us drop into Jupiter where we would die? I don't understand their motivations."

Ignoring him, Juliette got up and walked into the hall. He was right about it not making sense. Where were they? The lights flashed off.

"Welcome to *the Progenitor of Torment!*" a horrid voice screeched over the intercom.

-2-

Ebuka slammed her fists against the walls of the Progenitor but to no avail. For some reason, she was unable to force her way through inches, maybe even feet, of hardened steel.

She wanted to panic and scream, to cry out to whomever could hear her and express her agitation, though the rational part of her knew that this would only be a waste of time. Would that bring the pod back? No. Would it bring her father out of prison where he belonged? Certainly not. It would only prove to her opponents that she was unable to control herself and that they had won; and since neither of those things were true, she refused to prove them right.

No, the rational thing to do would be to defer to the guards on board. They would understand her predicament and be able to help her return to *the Dominion*. They would be able to communicate with it and call down for another pod. Yes, that was the best option. Forcing herself to calm down with deep breathing, Ebuka turned around and made her way back to the waiting room.

It felt good to have not panicked; relaxation and focus were clearly the superior states of mind for dealing with crises. Briefly, she wondered why humans had evolved to resort to the former but didn't care enough to finish her train of thought.

Onward she walked, entering an endless shadow where there should have been a hall. Internally, she did a double-take. Questions about what had happened and if she was even going in the right place whirled through her mind, forcing her to question her sanity.

Eventually, she decided that it must have been the prison's fault. Ever since she had stepped aboard, it seemed as though nothing had gone right, except perhaps her conversation with her father. Other than that, evil after evil prevailed, leaving her lost and confused.

The darkness was not as endless as it had previously appeared, and before she knew it, Ebuka was standing underneath a flickering light. Around her, other lights started to follow suit, revealing the torture cells. Although this time, unlike the last time she had passed through, she couldn't quite see the prisoners. It was probably for the better, she guessed. After having been abandoned and left for dead by the warden, she didn't need to see the even more depressing sight of the inmates and the pain that they felt.

She found it odd how much lighting contributed to the mood that an area produced. Before, when she had walked through, she had experienced emotions of pity and sadness, wishing that she could have saved those who had been wronged. Now, she wished she could have still felt those things, but the tenebrosity precluded her from doing any such thing, and an anxious terror found its way into her mind instead.

Walking further still, with the hope that the waiting room would provide her with some relief from the unknown of the rest of *the Progenitor*, Ebuka started to understand that something truly sinister was happening to her. She was not so foolish to believe that all of these horrifying things were mere coincidences, and the fact that the warden would abandon her, proclaim that Ragnarok was coming, and seemingly be the one to send her to a ghost of a ship was likely no coincidence either.

It was strangely easy for her to admit that she had been set up from the beginning. She wasn't sure how, but that had to have been it. There was just too much that had fallen apart and in such a short period no less. It seemed likely that the warden was behind it; she just wouldn't have pegged him for the type of man to scheme. Perhaps she had only been unable to see it because of how intelligent he was, though.

She approached the door from the end of the sparsely lit hall, and only when she saw it, did Ebuka hesitate. Should she enter, or would that be the next step in the trap? *How paranoid I sound,* she thought, knowing full well that her newfound skepticism could be the difference between life and death.

From the distance, she could see guards standing around idly, likely waiting for her to attempt to enter, but she wouldn't fall for it. Especially not after the trickery that had already been used on her.

Once she got to the door, she ducked down under the window so that she couldn't be seen by those inside. It might have just been her paranoia, but she was starting to wonder if the people dressed as guards were even that. What if they were a part of whatever organization was causing Ragnarok? After what the warden said upon his flight from *the Progenitor*, it seemed incredibly likely.

What was she supposed to do, then? She wasn't much of a combatant, or effective at anything in the field. Her skills were far more intellectual.

Shut up, she thought, closing her eyes. She might not have been quite as athletic as some of the guards, but she was smart and resourceful. Problem solving was her profession, and all that she was dealing with was her largest problem yet.

Just like with any other problem, she needed to follow her normal procedure. First came the gathering of data, which would be crucial for understanding the context of the scenario. Second, she would research, or in this case, develop possible solutions in her head. And third, she would need to execute her ideas, probably to near perfection. It was just another day at work. Just another day at work.

As she was about to start gathering information, a loud clanking echoed around the ship. Ebuka felt the familiar feeling of panic rising in her chest and did her best to keep it down, informing it that it was not welcome in her body. She waited to see if any more noise would be made, but there was only silence. Whatever had caused that had been a one-time thing.

It was unknown and that fact scared her, but it was information, so Ebuka didn't complain. Maybe with a few other data points, she would be able to sort out what was going on. *One step at a time*, she thought. *One step at a time.*

An awful scream cut through the air like a bag of knives. She whipped around, unable to hide how terrified she was from herself any longer. How was she supposed to gather information in that environment? It was absolutely torturous, attacking her with silence and shrieks at the most inopportune times.

"I dance upon your grave as you watch, your face grave," a disembodied voice sang nearby. "While you protect yourself from the horrors, those you love will be dishonored! It will be glorioussss! Glorioussss! Come watch! It'll be oh, so fun!"

Ebuka knew that the demon was addressing her, that it was telling her to come, yet she refused to listen. She had decided at some point in her life that listening to crazy psychopaths wasn't the best idea, and it seemed like then was the perfect time to apply that wisdom to real life.

A cacophony of violence suddenly rang through the air, chilling Ebuka to the bone. She forced herself to her feet. It wasn't an amazing idea to wander through the darkness alone, especially if there was fighting going on. However, if she were to be found, she figured it would be better to be standing, so she could get away more easily.

With her ear close to the door, she could hear voices talking inside.

"She's probably still out there," one of them was saying. "She's stupid enough to just wander into a trap like this."

So I was right, then, she thought. In hindsight, all of the signs were pointing toward the fact that she was being ambushed, and she felt slightly embarrassed that she had been tricked in the first place.

"Should someone go out to take care of her?" one of them asked, and even Ebuka, who barely knew what was going on, knew that that was a bad idea purely based on the sounds that she had heard just a few moments prior.

"No, you fool," the other replied, as Ebuka would have. "Let's just sit tight and wait to hear from my father. This is all part of his plan."

It was at that moment that Ebuka wished she could have looked into the room to see who was talking. If the warden was the mastermind behind everything, she should have been able to look at the guard to see how similar they looked. If nobody looked like him, then she knew that she was wrong and it was not his son inside, speaking.

But even a single glance might have revealed her to them, so she stayed just out of sight of the guards. She heard footsteps within the darkness coming close to her, but not close enough for her to feel them. It was nerve-racking, and at that moment, she came to understand the idea of being stuck between a rock and a hard place.

Was it foolish to hope that she would be saved?

-3-

Juliette wished that she had been left alone in the darkness. It had been far too long since she had some good alone time, and she felt that it was due. Tim's presence only served to distract her from being able to fully clear her mind, and she couldn't forget about him because she could hear his breathing and the ambient light from the window presented his silhouette to her.

"We need a plan," Tim said, interrupting her thoughts.

"No! What we need is for you to shut the fuck up! I cannot stand how arrogant you are. I wish Ebuka were back. She at least understood me, but all you do is try to control me and tell me things that aren't true."

She felt a hand reach through the darkness and rest itself on her shoulder. "You're understandably angry," he replied. "It is important to recognize where that is coming from, though. Especially during a crisis like this."

She scowled and tried to break away, but his grip was like a vice.

"Are you truly angry with me, or are you finding it easy to use me as a target because there is nobody else around?"

Juliette's lips drew to a line. She refused to answer. He could hold her there as long as he wanted, but no matter what, she wouldn't engage. He was wrong, of course. He had to have been wrong. There was no way that she would be so rude as to irrationally direct her fury towards him even though he hadn't done anything.

All of her feelings were incredibly justified. She was angry because he wouldn't leave her alone, because he definitely thought that he was better than she was. She was furious because he hadn't been there sooner, even though he had known all of that about her father and family. She was enraged because he was not what he claimed to be, and dishonesty wasn't something that she could easily forgive. At least with someone like Jacques, even though he was an ass, she knew who he was. Hiding behind a mask was just something she couldn't stand.

"Would you like me to leave you alone?" he asked.

"Yes."

"I won't," he said simply. "I realize that this will only piss you off more, but during something like this, companionship can be the difference between life and death, and I will not be responsible for your death."

"If I go out there and die, it'll be my fault," Juliette growled, walking away from him.

"If you go out there and die, it'll have been my fault for allowing you to do so," Tim said, following her. "You don't know what's out there, and I can't tell you that either, but together, we're safer."

It was true, however, it wasn't something that Juliette wanted to admit. She wished that her mother would have been there for her to talk to. She knew she was acting erratic and that she didn't understand what was right and wrong anymore. She needed her anchors to keep her grounded, to remind her of who she was when she was down, but during her darkest moment, they had abandoned her. Perhaps that was why it was so dark.

"What do we do, then?" she asked, grateful that the shadows were able to hide the tears that had formed in her eyes after thinking of her mother. "How are we supposed to advance through life if we stop whenever we are met with an unknown?"

"That's the only time that we can advance," he replied.

Something about the quote felt oddly familiar.

"Do you think we should leave this office, then?"

"Yes," Tim replied. "There are those out there who do not have the same protections that we do. Shouldn't we help them as best as we can?"

"I'd rather live," Juliette said simply.

"This is a positive externality," Tim said. "Do you know what that is?"

Juliette shook her head, realized that he couldn't see her, and then said "no."

"It means that if we do something, the total benefits reaped will be greater than the effort we put in. So if you help these people, they will help humanity stay alive, meaning that your overall quality of life will improve, and you can achieve greater happiness."

"Not if I die," Juliette responded.

"Of course not. Nothing can happen if you die. I'm not saying there aren't risks involved with doing this; there are just high chances of great things happening. Although, on the other hand, if we do nothing, the death rates would likely either be higher than if we wouldn't have helped, increasing our chances of premature death."

Was what he said the truth? Juliette had no idea. She wasn't educated enough to disprove him, yet there was something in her gut that was telling her not to listen to him. He might know some things, but he was still unable to predict the future.

"I don't know what I want to do," she said after some thinking.

"Time is becoming a more and more precious commodity," Tim reminded her. "The longer we wait, the more haste we must act with."

Juliette sighed. Very rapidly, she was running out of reasons not to go. She wondered if she should mention how she was afraid after all that had happened, or that she honestly didn't even want to, although it almost felt as if that truth had been implied by her earlier concerns. He likely knew that she felt that way by then.

"We can go," she said, reluctant to the end.

"Good," Tim replied, not wasting any time and advancing into the hall outside of Ebuka's office. "First, we should go over what we know. And surprisingly, that's a lot more than nothing."

Juliette braced herself for some sort of impossible leap of logic that had nothing to do with reality. He had done that when talking about her father, so why not with something else as well?

"Second, we need to figure out what we can do with this information, and last, we need to execute that plan."

"You make it sound so easy," Juliette muttered, rolling her eyes.

"It's just a blueprint. So, from what we know, we can start with the decrease in gravity. That, as mentioned before, could only mean that the orbit has decayed. The interesting part with this is that the decay stopped, meaning the decay was either deliberately stopped and we arrived at our destination, or it was fixed.

"However, we can disprove that second theory, as our destination was loudly announced: The Progenitor of Torment."

Juliette widened her eyes in agitation. Would he ever be done talking? Would she be able to get a word in, or would their partnership just be that one-sided?

"That's a prison, right?" she asked, hoping that he would stop to listen to her.

"Yes, yes. Like Alcatraz from Old Earth." She was grateful he included that analogy, as she understood the history of Old Earth even better than *the Dominion,* so it made sense to her. "It was lowered to this point because the government didn't want the prisoners to have a chance of escaping. Now that we are docked with them, though, I wonder if perhaps all of the prisoners have already been freed and this was one of the later steps in a plan that we haven't been able to see initializing."

Juliette scratched her head because she was confused and it itched. "What would be the point in sending us to the prison, though?"

"Either to free the prisoners or to use them for something," Tim replied.

Suddenly, just how dark and quiet it was was impossible not to notice. Juliette couldn't help but wonder if they were alone in the darkness. At any moment, an inmate or guard could pass within inches of her, and she would have no way of knowing. In her mind, monsters spawned, destroying any final senses of security that she might have had. Staying and dying in Ebuka's office no longer seemed like such a bad option.

"Shhh," Tim whispered even though Juliette had already gone quiet. She bumped into his back an instant later, hitting the bridge of her nose as she did so. Her eyes watered frustratingly, although since it was pitch black now, it wasn't nearly as much of a problem as it would have been otherwise.

"There are others," he continued. "Can you hear them? Their footsteps and labored breaths?"

"Are they friendly or do they want to kill us?"

"There is no real way to safely find out," Tim admitted. "Especially not under the shroud of night."

"So what is our plan, then?"

"We need to find somebody who has better ideas than we do," Tim whispered, and if Juliette wouldn't have known better, she would have thought she had heard the hints of a chuckle in his voice.

"Congresswoman Abdullahi?" Juliette asked.

"Ebuka indeed," Tim confirmed. "After that, returning

power to lighting will be crucial to provide the public with some relief from their inevitable panic."

The public? Juliette thought. *We are panicking just as much!*

"Then, with the help of the reactors, *the Dominion* will be able to return to its natural orbit, and this can go down in the history books as an extremely terrifying, but ultimately dangerless event."

"You make it sound so simple," Juliette whispered. "It doesn't feel that simple."

"Solving problems rarely is," Tim admitted, "especially when they're this big. All we can do is take it step by step and hope that everything goes right."

"Do you have anything that can give us some light?" Juliette asked.

She heard Tim patting his body and then silence. "I have a flashlight on my tablet," he said once he was done. "Although it isn't a good idea to use it."

"Why not?"

"The light will only be a beacon for undesirables and those that might slow us down."

"But what if we find people that we can save, or it helps us get to Ebuka faster?"

"It won't," Tim insisted.

They heard a clanging nearby and at the same time, they both fell still. Juliette's mind raced, but she knew better than to speak than to ask any questions. Danger was far too close and strong enough that she knew any false movements or sounds would result in her death.

Something crunched and rolled towards them. It was too dark to see exactly what it was, yet that didn't stop Juliette from straining her eyes all the same. What could that have been?

Almost as if he could read her mind, Tim turned on the tablet at its lowest brightness and turned it towards where the sound had come from. Initially, Juliette had been relieved; it was just the helmet of a guard, after all. Then the light was able to pierce the darkness just a bit better, and she was able to see what had happened. A red trail followed the helmet, and it didn't take much for her to understand that she had just heard her third murder in as many days.

-4-

Ebuka heard footsteps approaching and knew that death would follow. In stories like hers, there were no happy endings. There were only cold, dark torture rooms from which she wished she could escape. She hadn't done enough good, saved enough people, to deserve anything less.

Moments before contact, a small part of her had hoped that the person coming to get her would be coming with the intention of saving her, although she knew that that wasn't the case, and it certainly wasn't the expectation.

So she wasn't exactly surprised when she started being beaten to death by an insane creature of the darkness. Blow after blow landed on her body, though she barely felt any of them. She felt strangely good, in fact, like an electric buzz was flowing through her veins. Not to say that the strikes didn't hurt, because they did, it was just that they didn't feel quite as damaging as she would have expected.

After some time, the buzz faded, and each blow brought with it a greater amount of pain. Up until then, she had made an effort to remain silent; her weakness was her own and she saw no reason to share it with others. It was only when she was unable to control it that cries of pain left her chest.

"Please," she groaned between strikes. "Please, stop attacking me."

The beast grunted and the next thing she knew, Ebuka was on its shoulder, being carried like a sack rather than a woman. Her whole body ached as if she had been slammed into by a space station, but Ebuka could tell that nothing was broken or even injured too badly. Whoever had attacked her had been intelligent or careful enough not to fatally wound her.

She tried to watch where they were going, but her eyes drooped and soon, sleep overtook her. The darkness was calm and safe, and she welcomed it a lot more than she would have liked to admit. In her head, she could find relief.

Standing atop the gallows, Ebuka couldn't help but wonder if she had finally gotten what she had deserved. The people had spoken, and what they had said might have hurt, but it didn't make their feelings any less valid. They hated her inaction and incompetency, and for that, she would pay.

If her sense of justice and service had been any less staunch, she might have fought back and defended herself from their attacks and insults. A tiny part of her was all too well aware of how irrational her constituents were being. After all, not only had they removed her from office, they had sentenced her to die as well.

An unknown rotten fruit slammed into her face, shaking her from her delusions that she might have been above such sentencing. She knew better than to reaffirm herself of good deeds that hadn't helped anyone. All that would do was cement lies in her mind, preventing her from being able to see the truth.

Horrid-smelling fruit streaked down her face, reminding her of the mask that she had put up to try to hide the rottenness beneath her surface. *If I hadn't been so terrible, then I would have done something for them*, she thought, eyeing the pitifully sad crowd that cheered on as they greedily witnessed her demise.

"GET HER OUT OF HERE!" a woman shrieked at the top of her lungs. She continued to wail but her voice cracked at one point and after that, no sounds came out of her emotionally charged mouth.

"You haven't done anything for us!" Juliette cried, standing near the other woman. "Look at all that we've lost, all that we've fought for just so we can be happy, and all that you've neglected! We are numbers. NUMBERS! You cannot even begin to relate to what it's like to be us. You are too disconnected to even care."

"End me," Ebuka whispered.

"You talk about so much, and yet, you do so little," a man said, continuing Juliette's rant. It took Ebuka far too long to notice that it was Tim, this time. "Your eyes might be big, but your stomach is so small that any amount of goodness makes you so nauseous that you avoid it like the plague. You disgust all of us."

"So end me, then," Ebuka said.

The crowd parted and her father came forward with the corpses of her mother and sister in his arms. "You talk so much of saving us, and here are your greatest failures. They are still dead, and although you didn't kill them, you were unable to save them. What use is power when it isn't used, when it is corrupted by the horrible people of the world like you?"

"SO END ME!" Ebuka shrieked. "PULL THE LEVER! You have broken my family, my trust, my spirit, the only thing left for you to break is my neck. So stop screaming at me and fucking do it."

The crowd went uncharacteristically quiet. Nobody so much as moved or even breathed. It was as if someone had taken a remote and paused the situation like it was a show that they were watching on television.

"You truly mean that don't you," an ethereal voice said to her.

"I do."

"Good. It's easier to elevate yourself from the bottom than it is from the top."

And everything faded to white.

Ebuka slowly sat up in the pitch black. Her body hurt more than she could have imagined, and when she tried to sit up and move, everything within her fought back, telling her to stay where she was. The pain was far too unbearable for such an action as moving her torso.

"Is anyone there?" she called out and immediately regretted it. Memories of being beaten flooded back to her, and she remembered how important it was to be stealthy. But what had happened between her being beaten and then? Where was she?

Her curiosity was overpowering, and she found herself on the verge of asking further questions. She was lucky that her survival instinct was stronger, though, and she refused to talk anymore.

Footsteps approached, causing Ebuka to involuntarily flinch and cover herself with her bruised arms.

"I wonder what I'll say to them when I get back," Ebuka heard. The sound was familiar, the phrasing even more so, and it took her no less than a second to realize that the person walking around was her father.

"Father!" she cried before she realized what she had done. Beneath the veil of darkness, her eyes grew wide and she sank back into the smooth wall behind her. It had been so easy to forget that he was insane. What if he was violent? What if he had come to kill her because he had forgotten who she was? The idea terrified her.

"I'll probably tell them all about my day at work," he continued, apparently unable or unwilling to hear what Ebuka had said.

In the distance, she heard another set of feet clanging against the steel ground. "After that, I'll ask the girls about how school went," her father said as he went off in the direction of the walking.

She heard the sound of someone getting punched and

found herself growing worried for her father's safety. He was strong, yes, but he was also insane. It wasn't safe to go into the darkness alone, especially not when there were other inmates out there.

"Maybe Ebuka has read a good book that she can tell me about," she heard next to her.

She blinked and shook her head in surprise. How had he done that? Wasn't he at the end of the hall, beating the other man to death? Being blind was infuriating, though it seemed as though she was the only one struggling with the absence of light. Was there something about insane people that made them good at navigating without the aid of their eyes?

"I want to tell her how proud I am," her father said rather randomly.

With all that had been going on, all that Ebuka had been feeling, even the most supreme of wills could not have held back her tears.

-5-

Jacques peered into the darkness of the Progenitor and couldn't help but feel jealous of all of the blood-thirsty creatures wandering through the shadows, killing anyone they came in contact with. The more he thought about death, the more his hands shook uncontrollably, reminding him of how long it had been since he had last performed a violent act.

He felt a sharp prick accompany a hand on his back and turned around to see the comforting face of his father. "You have been kept in a cage for far too long," the older man said. "I apologize for that, truly. You were never supposed to be anything but an agent of death."

Jacques growled, pulling out a pair of serrated knives as he eyed the door.

"I cannot, in good conscience, allow their hearts to beat while you sit here and lust for their blood. What kind of father would I be to see you suffer and support the source of it?"

Jacques' vision narrowed, and soon he was unable to focus on anything but the door in front of him. His breath gradually became heavier with each passing moment as predatorial saliva dripped down his chin.

"I need to maim them," he uttered with difficulty.

"I know you do," his father said. "I need you to as well. It will benefit all of us for you to. I apologize that I must ask you to wait only a moment or two longer, though. The effects haven't fully sunk in yet."

Jacques felt himself fade into his mind, only to be replaced by a monster. The monster was strong, stronger than anything

that it had ever known, and its proneness for violence far super-
seded anything that Jacques had ever experienced. It was a true
killing machine.

"Are you there, Jacques?" a man asked.

The monster growled, unsure why it didn't want to kill the
man. Perhaps it was the way he smelled.

"Go hunt," the man snarled.

Then everything went black under the veil of a bloodlust
so intense that the monster would have killed itself to satisfy it.

-6-

It was hard not to panic. Not only were they unable to navigate the darkness well, but they were also alone in it with a murderer. Juliette's first instinct was to bolt and lock herself in Ebuka's office, however the smallest bit of sympathy she had held her back; if she abandoned him, Tim would surely die. Well, that and the fact that she had forgotten where the office was. But that wasn't nearly as important in her mind.

Frozen in place, Tim and Juliette stood, afraid that any wrong movements might bring them to an untimely death. Her arms ached at her sides, which confused her as she was fairly certain that she had been able to exist without her body hurting before the lights had gone out. As quietly as she could, she crossed her arms in front of her to alleviate the discomfort in them, but even that was extraordinarily loud to the point that she thought she had exposed them to the killer by doing so.

However, when moments passed and she was still alive, Juliette found that now it was her feet that were beginning to ache. Moving would be far too dangerous, though, so Juliette willed herself to stand still as long as she could. This, of course, only pushed her to think about the pain in her legs that much more, making her inability to move all the more unbearable. It was quiet enough that everything from the sound of her breathing to her blinking seemed thunderous, forcing her paranoia to unknown heights.

Breathing echoed around her, and it took her a moment to realize that it was neither hers nor Tim's, but rather the other. The murderer. Her skin crawled at the thought of him and hearing that he might be within reach of her made her want to retch. The idea that somebody might want to kill someone for any reason at all didn't make any sense to her. It was truly the most horrible thing that somebody could do, in her opinion.

"I won't kill you," she heard in her ear. "I won't. You're safe. The other isn't."

Juliette opened her mouth to cry out to Tim, to warn him of the coming danger, but before she could say anything she heard a slash and a thump.

"No," she whispered. He hadn't deserved that. He might have been arrogant, but he hadn't been malicious or evil.

It might have been her imagination, but she could have sworn that she saw a silvery wisp trail through the void and exit the ship through the wall. Before she could wonder about what it might have been, she decided that she was most definitely seeing things after having such little visual stimulation over the past few minutes.

What was she supposed to do? How was she supposed to respond? She had been deemed worthy of life, but for what purpose? And if the murderer had been the one to say she was deserving of another chance, she wasn't certain that she even wanted to take it. What a tainted boon.

-7-

As much as Ebuka wanted to stay with her father, she knew that it wouldn't be productive, especially not if she wanted to prevent whatever 'Ragnarok-type' event was happening. Her change of heart had been quick and dramatic, beginning with the reminder that she was above self-pity and ending with the resolution that she was not so weak to believe that someone else would come to save her.

Instead, she had opted to take agency and go out and save the ship herself. She had no idea how to do that, of course, but she hadn't known what to do when she had first taken up the role of congresswoman, and she had already accomplished quite a bit, so it seemed that improvisation wasn't the worst thing ever.

Saying goodbye to her father wasn't nearly as hard as she had thought it would have been. The darkness helped with that, in truth; she didn't have to see his face nor was she able to think about the hurt way he might have looked upon discovering how she was abandoning him. It was their final goodbye, she knew, and somehow she felt whole instead of empty. Closure was a beautiful gift, and she had received her fair share.

A lump rose in her throat as she walked away from where he had taken her, and she came to understand that sometimes there wasn't a good option. The irrational parts of her brain gnawed at her intrinsic logic, feeding her lies about how she was an awful person because she was leaving her last living family member. Admittedly, the farther she got away from her father, the harder it was not to return. The voice in the back of her head had more influence over her than she would have liked.

Before long, she became overwhelmed with the fear that she might be lost. A void was her home, and within it, she was but a stranger, a visitor in somebody else's home. Reality dawned on her as she walked, telling her that no matter how hyped up she might have felt, and how excited she had been about saving people, none of that could account for the fact that she couldn't see.

It was impossibly demoralizing to have to walk from wall to wall, hopeful that she was navigating correctly. She imagined that if someone were watching her, they would be laughing at how idiotically erratic her movements were. It must have been so entertaining to witness. Feeling embarrassed, she hoped that nobody was able to see her.

Shut up, she told herself, feeling frustrated by the self-pity that she was experiencing again. It was growing old quickly. You're Ebuka Abdullahi. A girl that your father can be proud of. You don't get irritated when you can't do something; you work through it. Shut up and work, goddammit.

So she did her best to imagine the Progenitor in her mind so that she could lead herself back to where the pod had been. She realized now how foolish it had been to abandon that entrance in the first place, but hindsight was often clearer than foresight.

Surprisingly, with that image in her head, it wasn't hard to navigate back to the front of the prison. The pure blackness was almost helpful, forcing her to use her internal map instead of relying on any visual clues that might distract her. At certain points, she bumped into walls or corners, but soon enough she made it safely to where she had initially arrived at the prison.

She looked out the window of the dock outside the prison and saw a large mass floating through the blackness alongside *the Progenitor. Wait. Is that* the Dominion of Life? she thought. It couldn't have been. How had it fallen from such heights to be docked with *the Progenitor?*

Well, no matter. The 'why' didn't matter, at least not immediately. She just had to know what she needed to do moving forwards, and that likely didn't require much historical reasoning.

Using the same technique of picturing the station in her mind as she had done earlier, Ebuka crossed the border of the two stations and made her way toward her office. Why there, she didn't know, only aware that she had the most resources in that room than anywhere else, so it made sense to return. On top of that, it was likely that Tim was there or at least nearby, so she wouldn't be alone any longer.

During her travels, there were times that she had to stop because she was worried that she might have been heard or caught by someone else. There were times that she thought that she had been caught when footsteps got far too close, but she always ended up being safe.

How had the world fallen so far, from potential to hell? What had cursed them so? These questions could not escape her mind as she wandered through the void, only barely aware of where she was.

-8-

Juliette heard clicking and footsteps. She wasn't sure what either of those noises meant, specifically, but it seemed likely to her that they signified the murderer leaving. She breathed a sigh of relief and then collapsed to the ground. It felt good to relax, to be well and truly alone once again. She sat there for a moment to collect herself before taking the time to get back up and make her way to Ebuka's office. For some reason, it wasn't too difficult to find it if she closed her eyes and imagined that the hall was illuminated once again, and before she knew it, she was stumbling into the congresswoman's desk.

"Juliette?" she heard.

She whipped around fruitlessly, attempting to pierce the totalitarian darkness to find a light that simply wasn't there. "Who's there?" she asked.

"It's me," the voice said, and upon hearing it once again, Juliette knew who it was.

"Jacques?" she asked, suddenly feeling small. She had already been through so much and lost even more; she couldn't deal with him anymore.

"Juliette," he said once again, and a moment later, she felt the warm embrace of his arms around her. "I found you, Juliette."

Maybe it was her exhaustion, or perhaps she had needed to hear him say that for some time, but whatever the reason, she started to cry in his arms.

"Shhh," he said soothingly as he stroked her back. "Your pain will all be gone soon."

Ebuka knew before entering her office that somebody was inside. After being deprived of her sight for so long, her other senses, such as hearing and smell, were heightened. The scent of blood wasn't easy to miss.

As silently as she could, she walked into the room and made her way to her desk where she kept a pistol and a flashlight. Perhaps the other person was just a citizen looking for help from her, or maybe it was some monster that wanted to kill her. Regardless of the truth, it seemed like a better idea to be prepared to protect herself than the alternative, so she deftly removed both items from her desk and closed the drawer with the most amount of quietness that she could enforce.

The pistol felt awkward in her hand—it had been some time since she had shot it after all—but it still served to comfort her, if only slightly.

To her knowledge, the intruder was still unaware of her presence in the room, and the longer she waited, the less likely that was to be true. Her time was short and her patience for ignorance even shorter, so she worked up the courage to turn on the light as she leveled the gun around where a man's chest would be.

Taking a deep breath, no longer worried about whether or not she was found, Ebuka turned on the light. The result was momentary blindness as her eyes had dilated so much to absorb the barely existent light from the ship, so any stimulation was overwhelming. They adjusted quickly, though, and soon she was staring at a man with bloody knives.

"Hands on your head!" she screamed. "Drop the knives!"

The man, who Ebuka could now see was hugging a girl, pulled away and took a step back, but refused to listen to her requests.

"Ebuka?" the girl asked.

Ebuka froze momentarily, unsure of what was going on. "Juliette?" she said a second later. "What are you doing here?"

"I never left," the young girl responded.

"Step over here," Ebuka said, putting the gun down just enough so that it wasn't directly pointed at Juliette any longer. "Get away from him so we can talk."

"That's my husband," Juliette said as she shook her head. "I won't leave him."

"He's a murderer!" Ebuka said incredulously, doing her best to internally process the news that Juliette's husband was working for the organization that was behind Ragnarok. "You would protect somebody who has killed people?"

"I've heard a lot of lies today, but I won't fall for that one," Juliette said adamantly. "You and Tim are too similar, sometimes."

"What did he lie about?"

"He told me that my father had a part in all of this Ragnarok stuff," Juliette replied, her eyes growing red with emotion.

"How could he have known that?" Ebuka responded, wondering aloud more than she was asking Juliette.

"He couldn't. He had to have been lying. That's the only reasonable explanation."

Behind Juliette, the murderer shifted on his feet, clearly preparing to make some sort of move. *He's gonna kill her*, Ebuka thought. *He's gonna pounce, and if I'm not fast enough, he's gonna kill her.*

Just as she suspected, an instant later, the murderer jumped forwards, obviously trying to kill Juliette. Not wasting any time to think about the moral or legal consequences of her actions, Ebuka lined up the shot as best as she could with his head and fired.

She missed.

-10-

Jacques wasn't sure how it felt to watch Juliette's head explode in slow motion. On one hand, it was gloriously beautiful, red and white and gray streaking through the air in droplets and shards, but on another, it was horrifying. Jacques hated killing people with a gun. It was too fast and took away all of the pleasure that murder was supposed to bring.

Time returned to normal, and Jacques was left to stare at the corpse of his headless wife as it crumpled to the ground. "So that's what her life amounted to then," he said quietly. "Did she deserve death? Perhaps, but not by her hand. She didn't deserve something as awful as that."

"What are you talking about?" the woman with the pistol asked. Jacques' mind was still foggy from the drugs, but he was fairly certain that it was Ebuka Abdullahi.

"You!" he shrieked, furious that she had wasted someone in such a way. His mind was still foggy, but through the bloodlust he could vaguely remember why he was there. He had to assassinate her. She knew too much. If they failed, hell forbid, she would be the one to condemn them. She had to go. "I fucking hate you. You're an awful, pitiful excuse for a congresswoman. Look what you have done! Look at how you have treated this woman, my wife?!"

"I- I didn't mean to," Ebuka replied quietly.

Jacques knew that the pistol was trained on him, although he didn't care. He had power, after all. If need be, he could just slow down time and kill her.

"Remember, before this is all over, that like everyone, they chose us, not you. They hated what you gave them and applauded us for our tenacity, regardless of whether or not we actually gave them anything. That is what you can never possess."

Her finger twitched on the trigger, and he prepared himself.

"What is?" she asked, the fear shining through the thin mask that she gauchely wore.

"Faith."

And then there was a bang, and the world went black. *Did my power really fail?...*

-11-

irano sat in his dark office, crying. How could he have allowed such things to happen? Around him, his comrades sat, drugged and unconscious, incapable of fulfilling their oaths to protect the people of *the Dominion of Life.*

He could never understand why Tasvas or the monarch did the things that they did. They were cold humans, designed to lack ruth, whereas he was the opposite. He was a kind man who had joined the government to save people from events like Ragnarok.

So why are you doing all of this? he asked himself, only suddenly aware that he had never truly questioned his motives. Self-preservation had always been on the forefront of his mind, but the consequences of his actions had been noticeably absent throughout the time spent working with Tasvas. Did he really care more for his life than for his people?

It sickened him to think of such things. How easily he had turned against his convictions was awful. He was the police chief and a simple charlatan, who also happened to be a terrorist, had completely manipulated and controlled him.

Wiping the drying tears from his face, Girano reached into his desk and pulled out two things: a hand gun and a stimulant. The first would be for later, but the second he would have to use on his colleagues. He hoped that it would wake them up. He couldn't take Tasvas down on his own.

He prayed to God that the stimulant would work, and then pricked the first body he could find. Moments later, he heard them rouse from where they lay. He prayed to God that he might find the courage to kill a man, even if it was to save thousands of others. And most of all, he prayed to God that he wasn't too late, that his cowardice hadn't destroyed humanity forever.

-12-

*T*he Dominion of Life slowly rose to its original height as if nothing had gone wrong in the first place. Far below, *the Progenitor of Torment* orbited, empty of all of the prisoners and usurpers. It hadn't taken long for the course of history to right itself, and now Ragnarok was just a piece of human history.

If the engineers of *the Dominion* would have looked into the dead of night with any amount of interest, they would have noticed a few interesting things. Firstly, they would have seen that the Earth wasn't a frozen ball as they would have suspected. The heat from it was brilliant and bright, but it was too far away for the naked eye to think. How easily they discarded that planet that had once been their home.

More importantly for this, though, they would have noticed a pod escaping in the direction of Saturn.

And all in all, I want it to be known that I was right, as I usually am.

RESEARCH

Samson McCune

CONSTRAINTS AND INTRODUCTION TO THE PROBLEM

The basic idea for this project comes from the question "what would happen if the sun went out?" Of course, a simple answer would be that 99.9999% of all life on earth would die out, leaving the microbes at the bottom of the ocean as the only things that are able to stay alive. However, to propose the solution of death would be rather lame, so another idea will be explored—the idea of the deep space station.

To fully understand what this project will be detailing, it is important to understand what the constraints are. Firstly, the project will be avoiding super-structures like Dyson Spheres and stellar engines, since both of them rely on the power of a star, which we are assuming we will be without for an extended period. Secondly, the entire goal of the project will be to save the human race, and not to preserve all of the life currently living. Thirdly, this will be an exploration of new-ish ideas, so the Stanford Torus will not be considered for a possible design, mostly because of its popularity but also due to the Coriolis effect.

Immediately, it is easy to see that not only am I not an authority on these things since I am, in fact, a senior in high school, but these are also extraordinarily complex issues that are going to be attempted to be tackled.

These problems will be highlighted and resolved in sections with an ultimate design being picked at the end. Blueprints will be created and a general description of the science behind all of it will be included, with there only being holes when there isn't the science to support it.

THE POPULATION PROBLEM

The initial problem that would have to be dealt with would be the rapid drop in population that would be experienced. With the current infrastructure of humanity, the temperature drop would be bearable for a week or so, but after that, there would be an incredibly high death rate, especially in low-income communities which do not have the resources or means to heat themselves.

Perhaps the best way to model such a problem would be to use a logistic growth model, which explains exponential growth with a limited carrying capacity. It is often thought that humanity's population growth follows an exponential model, but it is likely logistic. The confusion comes because we have not yet found the carrying capacity of the earth, so it simply appears to be exponential.

The self-sufficient space station will not have such incredible carrying capacity, and as such, it will be important to accommodate this constraint. The problem that comes with a small size, however, is incest. Incest can destroy genetic lines, increase the chances of mental and physical illnesses that come as a result of genetics, and would be an incredible problem for a group of people that have to go to space. For this reason, the space station will begin with a population of 5,000 people and will enter a period of strongly encouraged reproduction if the number falls below 2,000.

The 5,000 people will fall below the inflection point of the logistic curve, which will expand after the production of the colony outperforms the consumption of the people. As of the beginning of the journey, the population cap will be close to

50,000 so that there is no amount of fear around extinction due to a lack of food and water before arrival.

In general, populations require a surplus of food to increase, so the biggest part of this will be to find a place that can be big enough to have a massive population potential and a huge amount of resources.

The Location Problem

One of the most important questions that must be answered is "where will humanity move?" This is a much more difficult question to answer than many would think. As is common for projects like this, liberties have been taken when assuming what kind of technology we have access to as people and what is truly possible to build. Fortunately, most of what will be mentioned is far closer to fact than fiction, meaning that objects such as warp drives will be avoided. Essentially, anything outside of our solar system has just been excluded from being a candidate for our new home.

Jupiter immediately stands out as the best choice, and with further research, it only solidifies itself as an ideal place to live in this exact scenario. This is because of a great many reasons, but it all essentially boils down to the fact that humans, like all other forms of life, need input, output, and a means of developing throughput.

The type and amount of resources available on and around Jupiter are truly astounding to begin with, dwarfing all of what we have on Earth. It has its core, its rings, and its moons all as contributors to our need for natural resources, and their combined masses make it inconceivable that we would ever use all of it up, especially with our diminished population.

The area around Jupiter is so monstrously huge that it wouldn't even be remotely foolish to simply blast our garbage into its atmosphere or space. On top of this, there is no life to pollute, with the only natural systems around there being the storms of Jupiter. This, combined with a few other variables which will be mentioned later, push the location outward, into an orbit that is within the rings of Jupiter.

Finally, the throughput comes into play and is the largest contributing factor to why Jupiter was chosen as the final destination for humanity. The atmosphere is 90% hydrogen, which is the main component used in nuclear fusion and will ultimately be the power source for the station. This might seemingly have nothing to do with throughput until it is considered how the inputs and outputs will be powered and developed.

But how will humanity *get* there?

THE TRANSPORTATION PROBLEM

As these problems are explored, transportation quickly becomes one of the strangest and most difficult parts of the process and is easily the most challenging part of the initial stages of this mission. With Jupiter being 629 million kilometers away at its closest distance, it is important to take into account the size of the ships that are taken, how long the journey will take, and the effects of deep space on the people within the ships.

This is where many liberties will be taken in terms of technology. Orbital mechanics are quite complex, so assumptions will be made that may be further from the truth than desirable. As will be discovered later in this project, the core assumption that must be made to make everything work is that humans have developed an extremely efficient method of performing nuclear fusion.

The crux of the following calculations is based on the fact that the starships that have been created are advanced enough to be able to generate 1g of thrust constantly for around a year. This sounds extraordinarily difficult, so it will be explained away by saying that the main focus of this project is the station and not the ships that are being used to go there. Perhaps with more time, this part can be amended and become even more accurate.

Kinematics and classical mechanics are friends. They understand this problem very well, and can tell us that with a constant acceleration of 1g, then flipping around to decelerate, it will take around 5 days, 16 hours, 2 minutes, and 2 seconds.

This is insanely fast and would be ideal for such an urgent task as the sun being replaced with a black hole of equal mass. To deal with the radiation, the ships will be armed with electromagnetic shields, meant to simulate the same effects that Earth's magnetic field has.

Upon arrival, each individual ship (of which there are hundreds), will receive instructions from a core ship that will explain to them which maneuvers to do to link together in orbit around Jupiter. The collection of these crafts will be the space station and will be known as *the Dominion of Life*.

THE POWER PROBLEM

It's easy to look at the things proposed and assume that they will never be possible with current technology. This much is true; current technology cannot output the amount of energy necessary to power this space station, to accelerate a ship at a constant acceleration of 1g, or to create the magnetic shields necessary to protect against the radiation of space. After all, taking less than 6 days to get to Jupiter is absolutely insane. With current technology, it takes 3 days to get to the moon, which is around 386,243 kilometers away from Earth for most moon missions, .061% of the distance to Jupiter when it is at its closest.

How is something like this going to be powered, then? Quick answer, nuclear fusion, as mentioned before. Long answer, this is almost a throwaway answer as the science is not yet there, so assumptions are being made to say that this could even be a possibility one day.

In theory, fusion can produce four million times more energy than fossil fuels can with an equal mass of both. This is an incredibly significant number, and coupled with the fact that fusion is a nearly unlimited source of power, it becomes even more insane to look at.

Now, the trip has been made and the station has been assembled. With nuclear fusion as the power source, the station will orbit outside the atmosphere of Jupiter. 90% of the atmosphere of Jupiter is composed of hydrogen, which is what stars us for nuclear fusion. With this futuristic technology, *the Dominion of Life* will be able to produce nearly unlimited energy by remaining just outside of the exosphere in orbit and dropping gas collectors into the atmosphere for production. It will be constantly consumed, and the result of the reaction, helium, can be used for cryogenics or other heat maintenance throughout the station.

THE GRAVITATION AND DESIGN PROBLEM

Gravity is one of the most interesting things to develop artificially and is what a lot of science fiction novels and stories get fully wrong. This fundamental force of the universe relies on mass, and with what is known about physics right now, creating artificial gravity so that a specific side of a box in space is 'down' is completely impossible. However, creating an acceleration that is not reliant on mass, but rather force, is much much easier, so this will be the method used.

The Dominion of Life will fit together like pieces of a puzzle to form the larger station. Walls will fall away procedurally to open up a flat area where people will live. There will be ecosystems and communities, and all in all, it will almost feel like Earth.

Flat surfaces like this are notoriously awful at creating gravity on their own, or at least a significant amount that will affect those near it reliably, so there must be something to generate gravity on the station. In this case, a decaying orbit with counteracting thrusters will be used. The sky, or up for the inhabitants, will be aimed into space, and Jupiter will be down. For this to have 1 g of acceleration being applied at all times, the station must be in a decaying orbit that provides for its elevation to be changed at 9.8 m/s/s. With the gravity of Jupiter being 25.9 m/s/s, this will not be difficult to find. To make the elevation stay the same and for *the Dominion of Life* to remain in a stable orbit, thrusters will be keeping it up and will, again, be powered by nuclear fusion.

THE PRODUCTION PROBLEM

For populations on *the Dominion of Life* to grow, there must be a surplus of many things, but the most important are food and power. Food, because people need to have something to consume in excess, allowing for more people to consume, and power for there to be room to expand to allow for population growth. In this case, the most important things are ultimately efficient energy transfers.

Ecosystems must be built, so specific areas of certain ships will be used to create wildlife conservancies and agricultural centers. They will be lit by artificial lights specifically designed to optimize photosynthesis. These will be large and will help to contribute to life support systems aboard the ship—covering anywhere from 52% to 60% of the space in the station—while also providing humans with a sort of natural world to experience apart from the metal box of *the Dominion of Life*. For this reason, glass panes will largely be used for the exterior so that people don't feel constricted by their homes.

To provide humans with a strong source of protein, there will be certain animals that provide us with meat, such as cows and pigs. These cattle will be grown on farms aboard the craft, which will largely resemble farms on Earth. It is evident, especially with this process, that the point of this mission will be to simulate experiences from Earth as much as possible while also being aware of reality.

The food will then be processed for human consumption, and the feces and other animal byproducts will be used to fertilize the plant growth so that this cycle will be able to continue on *the Dominion of Life*.

This covers the food, but the expansion of the ship requires a surplus of electricity and other resources as well. Of course, nuclear fusion will provide the excess electricity, but the rocks and minerals will be provided via extensive asteroid and moon mining. Jupiter has access to some incredibly massive repositories of stone, hydrocarbons, and metal in the form of its large moons. Ganymede, Io, and Europa will be the only moons that are required to mine from due to their incredible reserves of resources. For this mining, unmanned drones that can handle the more chaotic conditions of the moons will be used, meaning that the process will be automated. Human lives will not be risked here.

The station will be built such that further expansion is not only incredibly easy but also expected. Pieces will fit together easily with a base design and then will house agriculture, homes, workspaces, diplomatic areas, or leisure areas.

Something that has not been covered yet but is massively important to the development of a larger civilization is water control. If more water is required for more life to be created, missions will be sent to Europa for mining since it has an icy surface and an incredibly extensive subsurface ocean. From there, the water will always stay aboard the ship or in pods in orbit that can be easily accessed. The water will go through a filtration and waste management system after use and then be sent back to the station for reuse.

THE LABOR PROBLEM

The entire point of this ship is to imitate life on Earth as closely as possible, and this might be where exceptions to this rule are made. Simply put, labor aboard *the Dominion of Life* will need to be significantly different than Earth if the station is to remain operational. For example, in the United States, about 13% of the people work to produce goods, not including agriculture. 80% of people work in services, 1% work in agriculture, and 6% are self-employed or have another employment status, which includes unemployment.

The Dominion of Life cannot have such a large portion of the population working either for themselves or be without work. On top of that, there likely will be a new portion of the labor market that is dedicated to maintenance. Those working in maintenance will initially be engineers, specially trained in this field, but soon it will become easier to do these jobs with less and less education as the systems will be taught to children in their K12 years and the systems will be simplified so that they are more easily fixed by anyone.

Estimated, based on nothing but intuition, the service industry will increase to 85%, taking the self-employed and converting them to either maintenance or production to develop the infrastructure of the ship and ensure that it doesn't collapse.

THE GOVERNANCE PROBLEM

The problems thus far have been directed towards solving scientific issues due to the Sun going out, but this one tackles the government that will exist on *the Dominion of Life*.

In small communities, especially in drastic situations, forms of representative democracy do not work well. They are too slow and inefficient with their problem-solving, so catastrophe could likely occur before any sort of action was taken towards solving a problem.

For this reason, there will be a democratic monarchy, essentially with the leader of the space station as the lawmaker and the executor of the laws. In this sense, congress and the presidential position of the current system within the United States will essentially be merged. As the population grows larger, this power will be dispersed and a small congress will be formed. This will occur at an exact population value, which will be determined by far smarter political scientists aboard *the Dominion of Life* than I.

The judiciary will be an entirely separate body from the beginning and will be assigned based entirely on testing, which will include exams that attempt to measure impartiality. The judiciary body will consist of seven justices at the highest level and will expand if the population requires it. The point of this will be to create a check to the power of the monarch, so the monarch will not be able to directly alter or harm the judiciary itself. Once the population grows larger, there is a higher chance of corruption, so congress will begin to check and balance the courts, acting as it currently does in the United States.

Other initial, important laws will be decided and voted on before the monarch is put in place. This would imitate the Bill of Rights and the primary goal of it will be to preserve culture as much as possible. *The Dominion of Life* will be a melting pot of the life of the world and there will be conflict and growth as a result of this development.

SOURCES:

"50/500 Rule." Encyclopædia Britannica, Encyclopædia Britannica, Inc., https://www.britannica.com/science/50-500-rule.

Admin. "Can Photosynthesis Occur in Artificial Light?" BYJUS, BYJU'S, 31 Mar. 2021, https://byjus.com/neet-questions/can-photo-synthesis-occur-in-artificial-light/.

"Advantages of Fusion." ITER, https://www.iter.org/sci/Fusion.

"Employment by Major Industry Sector." U.S. Bureau of Labor Statistics, U.S. Bureau of Labor Statistics, 8 Sept. 2021, https://www.bls.gov/emp/tables/employment-by-major-industry-sector.htm.

"Europa." NASA, NASA, 4 Nov. 2021, https://solarsystem.nasa.gov/moons/jupiter-moons/europa/in-depth/.

"Helium." Encyclopædia Britannica, Encyclopædia Britannica, Inc., https://www.britannica.com/science/helium-chemical-element.

Holly Otterbein | Published Oct 20, et al. "If the Sun Went out, How Long Would Life on Earth Survive?" Popular Science, 22 Mar. 2021, https://www.popsci.com/node/204957/.

"How Long Would It Take to Get to Jupiter? • the Planets." The Planets, 10 June 2020, https://theplanets.org/how-long-would-it-take-to-get-to-jupiter/.

"Home, Space Home." NASA, NASA, https://science.nasa.gov/science-news/science-at-nasa/2001/ast14mar_1#:~:text=Titanium%2C%20Kevlar%2C%20and%20high%2D,orbit%2C%20minimizing%20 weight%20is%20crucial.

Hudy-Velasco, Oseas. "Electromagnetic Radiation Shield for Space-craft." ScholarWorks at WMU, 17 Apr. 2018, chrome-extension://efaidnbmnnnibpcajpcglclefindmkaj/https://scholarworks.wmich.edu/cgi/viewcontent.cgi?article=4014&context=honors_theses#:~:text=The%20Earth's%20magnetic%20field%20protects,charged%20%20particles%20%20towards%20the%20%20poles.

Jenkins, James, and HopDavid. "How Fast Will 1G Get You There?" Space Exploration Stack Exchange, 29 July 2013, https://space.stackexchange.com/questions/840/how-fast-will-1g-get-you-there.

Let's Talk Science, and July 23. "Escape Velocity." Let's Talk Science, 23 July 2019, https://letstalkscience.ca/educational-resources/stem-in-context/escape-velocity.

"Major Land Uses." USDA ERS - Major Land Uses, https://www.ers.usda.gov/topics/farm-economy/land-use-land-value-tenure/major-land-uses/#:~:text=About%2052%20percent%20of%20the,%2C%20and%20farmsteads%2Ffarm%20roads.

Rome, Len. "Going to the Moon? Find out How Long It Will Take." WYTV, WYTV, 6 Apr. 2021, https://www.wytv.com/news/daybreak/going-to-the-moon-find-out-how-long-it-will-take/#:~:text=Most%20lunar%20missions%20have%20taken,an%20how%20to%20get%20the.

Tillman, Nola Taylor. "Asteroid Belt: Facts & Formation." Space.com, Space, 5 May 2017, https://www.space.com/16105-asteroid-belt.html#:~:text=Composition,tend%20to%20contain%20more%20ices.

Tillman, Nola Taylor. "Jupiter's Atmosphere." Space.com, Space, 18 Oct.

2018, https://www.space.com/18385-jupiter-atmosphere.html.

US Department of Commerce, NOAA. "The Planet Jupiter." National Weather Service, NOAA's National Weather Service, 26 July 2018, https://www.weather.gov/fsd/jupiter#:~:text=Atmosphere%20 and%20Weather%3A%20Jupiter's%20extremely,Jupiter%20 also%20me%20the%20Sun.

Zimmermann, Kim Ann. "Jupiter's Moons: Facts about the Largest Jovian Moons." Space.com, Space, 1 Oct. 2018, https://www.space. com/16452-jupiters-moons.html#:~:text=This%20moon%20also%20 has%20sulfur,outward%20from%20Jupiter%20is%20Europa.